THE ENGLISH DRAGON BOOK 2

KATHI S. BARTON

World Castle Publishing, LLC
Pensacola, Florida
Copyright © Kathi S. Barton 2017
Paperback ISBN: 9781629896199
eBook ISBN: 9781629896205
First Edition World Castle Publishing, LLC. January 23, 2017
http://www.worldcastlepublishing.com
Licensing Notes
Cover: Karen Fuller
Editor: Maxine Bringenberg

CHAPTER 1

Rett needed a break. It was that or he was going to break someone. He stretched his neck muscles, hearing them pop and crack, and smiled when the man across from him seemed to freeze up for several seconds. Leaning onto his desk, he was glad to see the man back away as far as his chair would allow.

"I've not asked you for a great deal of money, Mr. Welsh. Only enough to see me through this hard time. You'll pay for the retraction or things will not go as you had hoped they would." Mr. Ralph — Douglas, he thought his first name was — smiled at him. "It matters very little if it's true or not. People will have it in the back of their mind for all time. Every time something else is written about you, even if it is true, they'll think of this. So, you pay me, then I'll see to it that a retraction is printed, not that it will do you much good. You're about as done in as they come, I think."

"You are right about that and more. But even had you only asked me for a dime, Dougie, you wouldn't have gotten it. I don't do well with people who blackmail me. And in the event you've missed reading your own papers of late, I'll let you know something that the entire world probably knows. I don't have any money. Not even the dime that you might have asked for." Dougie said his name was Douglas. "Well, when you come to my office, making demands that piss me off, I need to find some pleasure. And shortening your name gives me that. Now, as I was saying, Dougie, I don't think you understand the consequences of pissing me off."

"What are you going to do, Everettey?" For some reason his comeback about his own name was funny to him. "What do you think people will say when I tell them that you've threatened me? I will too. I'll do whatever it takes to get you to pay me. Do you think they'll come running to your aid? I think not. They'll say you're the monster that I've portrayed you as. Just pay me the money, I'll put in a retraction, and then things will be good for us both. For a while anyway." Dougie laughed again. "You just never know what might happen if I find I like getting money from jerks like you. But the article as it stands will run regardless of your opinion of me or what you call me."

Rett's phone ringing startled him and Dougie. Instead of telling the man to fuck off, which he really wanted to do, he picked up his phone. The laughter at the other end made him smile. There was only one person in the world that laughed like that. It was his good friend, Danburn.

"I'm wondering if you'd like to come and spend the holidays with us. We're going all out this year. Mother has even gotten some of the staff to.... What's happening?" Rett laughed. Even to his ears it sounded bitter and cold. "Tell me what's going on, or so help me, I'm coming to get you. You've had enough crap going on for several lifetimes."

"I have at that. But right now, I have a man in my office that is blackmailing me. And the really strange part of it is, he's thinking he's going to get money from me. Apparently, he thinks that I'm going to just bend over and take it up the ass. Would you like to buy a newspaper and get me out of this shit?" Danburn asked him the name of the paper. "The Centennial. You've heard of it. It just ran your marriage announcement. Which I hate that I had to miss, but with money being tight and all.... Well, I'm even further down on my luck than before with this jackass here."

"Hang on. Let me do some checking."

The man across from him looked at his nails, then brushed off something only he could see from his pants. He was trying to act as if he had not one care in the world, and Rett had a feeling that he didn't. The man was used to getting his own way in this sort of thing.

When Danburn came back on the line several minutes later, gone was the laughter and in its place was the man he knew could be as hard as nails.

"Put Mr. Ralph on the phone, please. I'd very much like to speak to him." The laughter and humor were gone, and in their place was the man that frightened him a little, even through a phone connection.

Rett just handed Dougie the phone without a word. He had no idea how Danburn knew who was in his office or who he had talked to while he held the line. But when Dougie whimpered and stood up, Rett got up as well to get himself a bottle of water. It would be like his friend to make someone shit themselves even over the phone.

Without a word to him, the phone was laid on the desk

and Dougie left. When he picked it back up, not only was Danburn talking, but a woman was speaking as well. It had to be Danburn's new wife. And she was having a good time with whatever was going on at their end.

"Thank you, love. Now we only have to get Rett here and things will be so much—" The woman's voice again. Rett wasn't quite sure if she was pissed or laughing, but Danburn growled low. "If you do that, then I will spank you."

"Danburn?" The laughter again, and this time it made him laugh as well. "I'm only assuming that you're speaking to your lovely wife, and she thinks whatever you did to Dougie was wrong."

"She spoke to him, made him tell her what he was up to. I did not. She's very good at that, making people tell her the truth when all they want to do is lie to me. What a world we've come to, don't you think? Where the first thing people want to do is lie to you. Sad is what it is, just sad." Danburn laughed. It was something that he'd now heard his friend do several times in the last several moments. A thing that Rett hadn't done himself in a very long time before now. "Come here to stay a few days. A month. Hell, for the rest of your life. I miss you. And I need your help."

"I've got to work. Unlike some people who own the world, I need to pay my bills and eat. And my mom's bills too. Apparently, my dad hadn't been…never mind. You only need to become your other half and feed yourself by gorging on fresh fish. Which, I will say, is much too fresh for my tastes." He leaned back in his chair. "I miss you as well. And I'm sorry I couldn't come for the wedding. I would have loved to have met your wife. But as I said, I can't right now. I have a lot of things riding on me having a job, even as piss poor as it is."

"She regrets it too. The not meeting you part...she loves being my wife." Rett would just bet she did. "Like I was saying, I need you for a few things. A good attorney is hard to come by, and you're the best. But I'm sending a plane for you now. You'll be on it or so help me, Rett, I'm going to become my other self and come there for you. I'm sure that won't go over any better for you than the now dead article in the paper."

The article. He'd completely forgotten about it in talking with his friend. Dougie said that he was going to have an entire story printed up that told all about his family. Some of it would be true...there had to be a kernel of it to make people believe the rest. And if he was honest with himself, he would have thought the public had all they wanted on him and his family. But Dougie had pointed out — and he might have been right — that a scandal was what people craved. Even when it was a lie.

"Did you buy it? The newspaper? Did you buy it?" He told him he already owned it. "It figures. You own everything, my dear friend. But this thing, I can't believe he thought that he could get anything out of me. Danburn, they think I'm rich. Everyone does when they hear someone is an attorney. I'm not. Why would someone come here, say that I'm some sort of asshole and killer, and expect me to come up with forty million dollars? I don't even think there is forty dollars in my account, much less forty million."

"I'm sorry, buddy. I truly am. I've been reading up on your dad's ordeal again, and your mom's predicament as well. You should know that I wish I could have been there for you from the first, but I had no idea at the time that it was

9

you. But I have good news. I need you to come and work for me, Rett. I've asked and asked, but now I need you here." Rett closed his eyes. He knew Danburn was serious, but he had no idea of the obligations that held him here. "I'm sending the plane and my wife to get you. When she gets there, you'd be best served to do as she says. She's not a nice person when she doesn't get her way."

"I bet she would have to be hard being married to you. But I just can't do it, Danburn. I've told you this before, I'm broke. I have vacation left but if I quit, I'll even lose that. I have no money to take off even if I wanted to. I don't even have.... Hell, Danburn, I don't even have a pot to piss in right now." He told him he knew that. "You would. I can't swing it without things falling apart here. I've told you that. I'm supporting my mom and myself pretty poorly right now."

"I'm going to help you. And so you know, my wife is on her way." When the line went dead, Rett put the receiver in the cradle.

He wanted to cry. Turning his chair so that he faced his tiny window with the worst view ever, Rett was tempted to jump. He was sure that he'd live. That his broken body would be on life support forever and he'd be even more broke, if that was possible, than he was now. All he had was his name, one that used to mean things. Now it only meant ruin.

Rett—Everette Welsh the third, to be exact—had gone to college with Danburn. Not with him, really, but they met there. While he had struggled to study, Danburn had cruised. When things came up, like fees and such, Rett had taken a second job. Danburn had just pulled out his credit cards. The man had it all, and Rett had been in awe of how mature, how

10

smart, the man had been. Then he found out the truth. They weren't friends then, only acquaintances really.

Danburn was in his study group, not that he ever showed up for them. They shared a table together in lab too, and had spoken during class. That had been the extent of their conversations and friendship until one night, when he'd been invited to his home for a dinner party for Danburn's mother, Elissa. Two men who were as different as night and day in the same house.

The dinner was far better than anything he'd had in a long while. The courses were perfectly timed, the wine flowing. As he sat there with Danburn and his mother, they all talked about not just college, but Danburn's other home, the servants that had come here for the party, and the things they were going to do when they graduated in a few months.

He'd known very little about the big man. It wasn't until about halfway through their first year that he realized that not only was Danburn a truly nice guy, but he wasn't human. He'd told him — during a bitch session — that he could change into a dragon. A big fucking one, he'd told Rett. The night of the dinner, he got to see him in his full glory.

It was that part, the man shifting into a large dragon, which had startled him out of the house and into oncoming traffic. Rett had thought, but knew better now, that Danburn had been trying to fob him off, get rid of him with this ridiculous story throughout their college years. But the car that had hit him nearly killed him, and brought the two men together in such a way that Rett still wondered about. It was then that he met the other people that Danburn had called friends too, each of them dragons in their own right. And Rett had been

11

friends with them all since that fateful night.

Not that he thought Danburn had had anything to do with him being hurt. He knew it was his own fault, running away from words that confirmed what he'd been told several times over the years. Danburn had not left his side the entire time Rett was in the hospital. And when he'd been released, his leg and arm in a cast, Danburn had brought him to his home, a larger one than most of the dorms that he'd not been able to afford, and helped him catch up with his classes. That was when he'd learned that not only was Danburn a dragon, but he was older than anything Rett had ever known. And much better off than Rett could have ever in all his life imagined.

"I don't need the education. As I have told you, I'm not human. But I'm not in my twenties either. I'm old enough to remember things that even history books no longer cover. The money that I have, it's from my family. So far back now that I doubt even my mom knows who started the first savings account that put us where we are now." Rett had nodded then, not sure if he wanted to know it all. "You have questions?"

"Too many to put out right now. You're a dragon, I know that, but are there more of you? I mean, your mom for sure, but others too?" Danburn nodded and told him he knew two others. Hanson McClain and Kip Newton. "How am I supposed to believe that, Danburn? I mean, I know you showed me, so I know that you're not lying, but I have to admit, it's a lot to take in. Especially for me, when I've never even thought of dragons."

"Would you like for me to show you again?" Rett said no, that once was enough. "You're a good man, Rett. A better friend too. And the reason that you've never thought of dragons is because we like to keep it that way. For humans not to ever get it in their heads that they have to be out hunting for us like they used to."

"All right, I guess I can understand that. I mean, you hear about…I guess I never thought that part was true either. That there were dragons that flew the sky." He looked around the room, then at the books that he'd been studying. "Why are you doing this for me? I'm not in your league of…well, anything. Why?"

"You're a good man, as I said. And you're going to make a great lawyer someday. I think, sometime down the line, I might need you to come and rescue me from myself." Rett told him about his money worries. About his family and father. "I've taken care of your money issues at the college. There isn't much I can do about the rest, I'm sorry for that. But the other…well, it's the very least I could do after what I made you do by running from me. You won't have to work anymore to go here, either. There is a fund set up for you to use for housing and food."

"I don't want you to do that." He told him it was done. "Danburn, you don't know me. For all you know, I could be this guy who scams people all the time. I need for you to stop this now."

"I trust you more than with my life, but those of my friends and family as well. Besides, it's done. And someday, I don't know when, I might need you to come help me. I'd like for you to think of this as a loan, one until you can repay me with assistance." He nodded, unsure how that was going to work. "Rett, I swear to you, I will never ask you for anything that you aren't willing to give."

As the years rolled by, he studied like it was his job. At first, he'd not wanted to take help from the other man, but he needed it to make it work. His name, the Welsh name, hadn't been much in a long time, but it got worse once he was out of school and trying to make a name for himself. Rett looked up from his musings when someone touched his hand.

"Mr. Welsh, Mr. Peashaw would like to speak to you." What now? He wondered. But instead of asking, he told Mary that he'd go. "I don't think he's very happy."

"Do you know what's going on?" She shrugged and he smiled. The girl was as shy as he was when it came to making friends. "I might need some empty boxes with the way my luck has been going of late. I don't know what he might want, but to be called to his office like this, it can't be good."

"You'll be all right, I know it. You're a good attorney." He nodded. Rett *was* a good attorney, he just worked for shitty people. "Go on now. See what he wants. Maybe he has a promotion coming up."

Not likely, but he made his way to the tenth floor. If Mr. Peashaw could have managed it, he would have had his offices on the roof, just so he could have the highest level to look down on people. Rett had disliked the man since he interviewed with him all those years ago, but he had taken the job when no other offers were forthcoming.

As he knocked on the door, Rett ignored the secretary at the desk. She was as snobbish as Peashaw was, and even if he were to ask her a question, she'd just glare at him. He figured that was her task, to put people in a bad mood *before* they entered the office. Rett realized how much he really hated his job.

The room, when he was allowed entrance, was just as it had been all those years ago when he'd interviewed with the man. The walls were dark, the furniture too, and the carpet was a blue so dark it looked black. Not even a dust mite dared mar the surface. The books, all of them as old, or older, than Rett was at thirty-two, were dark with age and unused. It was like being in a cave. Or a haunted house. He sat down when told to in the most uncomfortable chair he'd ever put his butt in.

"Mr. Welsh. What do you have to say for yourself?" He had plenty to say, he supposed, but nothing that Peashaw wanted to hear. Of that he was positive. "I've just gotten off the phone with the local rag, The Centennial. They're saying that you've threatened one of their staff."

"I don't think Mr. Ralph was actually working there. But yes, I did in a way. But not until after he threatened me. He was printing an article about me that wasn't true." His boss stared at him. "He put in there that I was a murderer, and I'm not."

"Might do you some good to have a wife. She'd keep you cleaned up if nothing else." Rett didn't even bother looking down at his worn and old suit. He had no idea where his comment had come from, but it was a moot point he supposed. It was probably in reference to his own wife and how, rumor had it, she picked out everything the man wore, including his underthings. "But we don't like to have our people threaten anyone. You'll apologize this moment and take out an ad in the paper stating that you were wrong."

"I'm not wrong. I think I'd remember if I had murdered someone, don't you think?" His boss asked him if he was

15

trying to be funny. "No, but I don't think I should have to tell someone I'm sorry for him lying about me. And, well, if I apologize, it looks like I am someone that would kill for no apparent reason, and I'd never do that. I don't think I'd ever murder a person for any reason, as a matter of fact."

"I don't see what one thing has to do with the other. Just man up and do what I said." He started shuffling the papers around on his desk, dismissing him, Rett knew. "I'll expect to see it in tomorrow's edition. That'll be all."

"I quit." The words spilled out almost too quickly. Rett looked at Peashaw when he finally looked at him, and could see that he was just as shocked as Rett was. But when the words hung there, just for a moment, Rett realized that's just what he wanted to do. "I can't be subjected to a firm that won't back up someone that's been here for as long as I have. I will turn in my resignation before I leave for the day."

"And what will you do, Welsh? Run your own firm? You don't have the money to get your rent paid on time since your father killed those two people and left you high and dry. Why, your mother is calling here every week wondering if there is some delay in your pay so that she can get her part of it on time." Mr. Peashaw shook his head and went back to shuffling papers. "You are no more quitting than I am. Get back to work, and like I said, have that apology in the paper tomorrow."

"No." Rett was feeling better with every word. "I'm not going to do that, and I'm not going to work here any longer. I've had enough, and I think this is the best thing I could do for myself. My mother will have to.... Well, I'll survive this. As I have a great many things in the past, I suppose."

Before he could change his mind, he left the office. On his way back to his desk, he thought of all the shit this was going to do to him. How hard it was even now to make the threads of his life meet. But he wasn't going to stay here. Not any longer. And that alone gave him a little more bounce in his steps.

It took security ten minutes to make it to his desk. He had already told Mary what he'd done, cleaned out his desk, and had his equally threadbare coat on. It was terrifying to think he was out of work, but it was also the best feeling he'd had in a long time. He was standing on the sidewalk when it hit him. He was no longer employed.

Going to his apartment, Rett set his things on his table and sat down. He didn't have the slightest clue what he was going to do now. There wasn't much in the way of food in his house, no stash of money to lean on when things got tough. Things were always that way for him, it seemed. And he had no idea what his mother would think. The worst, no doubt.

As he sat down to a bowl of cereal, the last good meal he would have for a while, he thought of nothing but putting the food on the spoon and getting it to his mouth. He was nearly done with it when someone knocked on his door.

He could only stare at the beautiful woman standing there. She had a coat in her hand that looked entirely too large for her, and a smile that not only put him at ease but made him smile back at her.

"Hi. It's chilly out, isn't it? I forgot my coat, and this was on the plane. I think it belongs to Danburn." The woman standing at his doorstep took his breath away. He knew who she was, Danburn's wife, but for the life of him, he couldn't remember her name. "Kendrick. Danburn told you I was coming. I'm here to take you back with me."

"I quit my job today." She grinned at him. "I don't know why I did that, but I'm in deep shit. But I'm free to come for a visit now, I guess."

"Great. We'll be glad to have you, for as long as you want to stay. But as far as you being in deep shit, I don't believe that either. From what I've been told about you, you're a very resourceful man." Rett told her that Danburn always said that. "And I'm sure he's right. Well, since you have no ties here now, you can pack up and come with me. The plane is waiting for us. Someone will come here and close up for you too. I've already arranged it."

"Why?" She told him that she knew she'd be able to talk him into coming with her, and didn't want to chance him changing his mind. "No, I mean, why are you wanting me to go home with you? I don't know what Danburn told you, but I'm not really the type of person he hangs around with."

"I'm not the type of person that one like him marries either, but here we are. And I've been where you are right now. Broke, no hope, and nothing to show for all the hard work you've put in." He nodded before he could think that wasn't something he should share. "Come on now, Rett. Let's get you going before Danburn comes too."

He wasn't sure how it happened, but within an hour not only was he going with her, but they were having dinner on a very expensive plane. Rett also found that he really liked Kendrick English. She was a perfect match to his friend the dragon.

~~~

18

Cassie walked the hallway once more, just to make sure there was nothing out of place. She'd been doing that all day, just taking a trip down hallways to make sure it was ready to open in a couple of days. She wanted things to be perfect.

Three weeks ago, she'd found herself on the doorstep of Danburn English. She knew what he was. His dragon, larger and stronger than her own, had called to hers. As soon as she met him, Cassie wanted to leave the area immediately. When she'd first met him she thought...well, he wasn't a mean person, just not...kind, she supposed she'd call him. Then she'd met Kendrick.

"I need someone to work with me. Not behind me, but right beside me. I know that you're a dragon, and I could also use some help with that as well." Cassie had nodded, then shook her head. "You don't want to work with me? Well that sucks. I thought we could be a good partnership or something."

"I don't want to work for anyone. What I mean is, I don't have to work, not really. I have money, a great deal of it, but I can't get to it. I might not ever be able to, honestly. My father is holding it over my head. I'm only here...well, I'm here because I have no place to go and my dragon needs to submit to Lord English's while I'm in the area. I know that I'm babbling, and I'm sorry about that, but I've been having some trouble lately and.... Well, let's just say that while I'm here, I'm under Danburn's rule." She asked her why her father was doing that. "I suppose because he can. He is not a nice person at all, and has it in his head that women, all of them, are only good for a couple of things. Mostly to cater to his needs. It's not his money, but mine. However, because of the laws of our kind, he can pretty much do what he wants. I have no mate that can, I guess, take over his duties of making my life a living hell on earth."

"That's the stupidest thing I've ever heard." Cassie agreed with her, but said it was the way they'd done things for centuries, and she was just a lowly female in the eyes of the laws of their kind. "I don't believe that any more than you do. I'm going to have Danburn look into this for you. There is no reason for you to be homeless and without money when you've got it."

Four days later, not only did she have her money, but her dad had also given her some of her other things. Like the jewelry her mom had left her, as well as a few other things, personal ones that Cassie thought she'd never see again. Cassie went to Danburn after her things had been delivered by a large van and asked him what he'd done.

"I did nothing. My wife did." She looked over at the small woman, then back at Danburn. "In the event you don't know this yet, Kendrick isn't a pushover, nor is she one to be ordered around. I think your dad figured that out pretty quickly when she spoke to him. By the way, there are a few more things coming your way too, items that I only just found out about. He will turn them over to you."

"Thank you very much. I never...he gave me my money. All of it. And my mother's jewels as well." Danburn congratulated her. "No, you don't understand. He told me that he'd sold them off. Took and sold them to a pawn shop a few years ago."

"Well, I'm sure that he's regretful for that as well, if that was what he actually did." Danburn had leaned back in his chair. "So now that that's settled, would you like to come and work for me? Mostly you'd be working for Kendrick, but I'd need your help on occasion too."

"Doing what? I just got out from under one bastard...I'll not work for another." He laughed, and she had felt her face heat up. "I'm sorry. I'm not normally so rude. I mean I am, but not to people that have gone out of their way to help me."

"That's fine. What the job would entail is you working with my wife. Kendrick doesn't want to be a housewife, and I don't blame her. It's very time consuming and we have staff. But what she wants to do is work with the homeless and find them shelter and a good hot meal. The building that we have renovated is done now. It only needs someone to keep things running smoothly. There will be people there to help, but you would be in charge." She asked if he normally indulged his wife. "You should ask her that. To hear her tell it, it's all I do. But I assure you, I can only do so much before she comes down on my head again. She isn't one to take fools lightly. And I do make one of myself where she's concerned."

"And you want me to come and work for you both. Doing what?" Danburn explained just what it was they needed her to do. "That's all? Just run the shelter for you and keep it in working condition?"

"Pretty much. I mean, I'm sure there will be pitfalls, but we have attorneys for that sort of thing. There will be a staff too, one that will report only to you. Also, I've hired a doctor and dentist, but I don't know them that well and hope that they'll work out for us. If not, then we'll do something else."

So here she was, working for a dragon and his mate. Cassie enjoyed it too. And working for the English's wasn't as difficult as she thought it might be. They were good people, very much in love with one another, and they treated her with respect. Two things she'd not had a lot of in her lifetime. But they were far from friends, she thought. He was her boss, as was his mate.

Cassie had just entered her office when she turned at the sound of her name. One of the people staying there full time, a helper of sorts, knocked before entering with her and closed the door behind him.

"There are two men at the door who are asking to speak to you." Cassie, as everyone there was calling her, asked who it was. "I'm not sure who one of them is, but the other one is Timothy Bond. He claims to be a friend of Lord English."

As she made her way to the front of the building, she tried to remember if she had any appointments today. There was no one that she could think of, but sometimes, not often, she'd forget to write something down. Or, Kendrick would set something up and forget to let her know. Cassie smelled the wolf before she got to the door and turned to Colin, the man who had come to her office, and told him to keep the cameras on the front of the place. She didn't want any trouble, but if there was, she wanted it recorded.

The doorway was open, but both men stood outside it. For some reason, she thought that she'd be better off just closing the door in their faces. Cassie didn't invite anyone into anything if she could help it. Vampires had a nasty way about them, and she wasn't sure she wanted to tangle with one today.

"May I help you?" The wolf turned to look at her. His eyes were a startling shade of purple, and full of anger and something more. She wanted to think she was wrong, but she thought he was insane. "We're not open just yet. And Lord English isn't around today."

"Danburn said he'd call you." She didn't say anything. He hadn't, and if this man thought she was going to fall for this, then he was dumber than she was. "I think you should check your messages. And if you can't read them, then find someone that can. I don't have time to be hanging out here while you try to do your job. Danburn is a very good friend of mine, and don't think he's not going to hear about this."

Pulling out her phone, because there had been times when she'd missed a call, she saw that she had not just a voice message, but also two texts. Reading them over before going to the message, she saw that Danburn had indeed let her know these men were coming. But she was to ask for identification.

After checking both men's credentials, she invited them in. The wolf, Timothy, told her to take him to the clinic with his friend, Walter. Walter, the vampire, was a doctor. Timothy.... Well, she had no idea what he might have done for a living. She thought it might be asshole, and if that was right, he was really good at his job. Before she could welcome them to the shelter, Walter looked her over like she was a bug on the wall. She disliked the man immediately.

"The next time we come around, I don't want to have to wait outside like I'm some sort of criminal. Be better prepared if you're going to work here." She didn't say anything, but he must have thought she needed more bashing from him. "You're not what I expected in a person running this place. I thought they'd be...I don't know, smarter. At least have a good deal more respect for those that are not just older, but much more experienced in the ways of the world. Next time, pay attention so we don't have to do this again."

"You mean like you're giving me respect? That's what you're talking about? Pardon me for saying so, but you're a dick. First class, but one all the same. So, fuck you and your getting respect from me." He just stared at her. "And for your information, I'm nearly twice your age, so you should have some respect for *your* elders, prick. Or someone might burn you to a crisp."

As she walked away, she heard him laughing. She had no idea why she'd done that—it wasn't like her to be so brash— but when she entered her office, Cassie called Danburn to be sure she wasn't fired after talking like that to one of his friends. He wasn't any happier with the man than she'd been.

"Neither of them are a friend. But Walter was willing to work at the clinic a couple of days a week as a physician until I can find someone else. Timothy is…I'm not entirely sure what his role there will be, but I've heard that he will be in charge of getting funding for the clinic and getting others to invest. I don't know either of them that well. But if you have to kick either of them out on their collective asses, I'll hold the door for you."

Casandra thought that might just happen, too. She told him what had transpired when they'd arrived and how she'd dealt with it. Danburn was both pleased and tickled that she could handle things there for him. As they hung up, she wondered what his wife would say, but realized that she'd more than likely agree with her. Kendrick wasn't going to take their shit either, Cassie thought.

CHAPTER 2

Rett liked the castle. He'd never been in one before, but he was pretty sure that there wasn't another as well maintained as this. And it was up to date on all manner of electronics, as well as Internet. He pulled out his ancient laptop and waited for it to boot up while he thought of the conversation he'd had with Kendrick when they'd been flying here on the English family jet.

"We need a personal attorney working for us. Someone to keep us out of prison for spending money on things like the clinic. Also, if you would, maybe you could work a couple of hours a week at our homeless shelter. It's not open just yet, but I would imagine that there are all kinds of things you could help some of the people with." He asked her if she knew of any other attorneys she could hire instead of him. "I don't want to hire anyone else but you. And I'm sure that Danburn knows a lot of people, but we wanted you. I'm just glad to not have to worry about it for now. I'm sure that someday I'll need to, but for now, I'm happy with the way things are going."

"What I mean is, I'm sure that there are more qualified

attorneys out there. I've been one for a while, but mostly all I did was research for the more important people at the firm." She didn't say anything, but he could almost feel her thinking she'd made a mistake. "I'll be glad for the visit, Lady English, but you don't have to pretend to hire me to get me out there."

"Okay, first of all? I don't do anything I don't want to. I came here to hire you. And unless you tell me no, I'm going to assume that you've taken the job. Secondly, and this is the most important thing you'll learn about me, I don't bullshit. I can, I'm pretty good at it, but when it comes to matters of this shelter and the people there, I'm as serious as a dragon's breath being hot. Do you not want to work for us?" He said that he didn't think he was qualified. "You let us be the judge of that. You'll be staying in the castle with us for the time being. There are houses that we can help you purchase if you think that would be better for you. Whatever you want to keep you happy, I'm happy with. Danburn said that you were having some issues at home? Well, we'll help with that as well. I've already started someone looking into the deaths that your father went to prison for. As well as your mother. She's not really well liked, is she?"

"My mother thinks that I should have been right there beside my father in prison for what he did. And no, she's not a nice person at all. Not even on her good days." She asked him what he'd done. "Nothing. I was living at home when he was convicted, but I soon left there in pursuit of a career. My dad, he killed a woman and her child one night in a drunken rage. He and my mother fought a great deal, and when he lost the battle, as he called it, he would go to the local bar and drink his sorrows away. I guess that's what happened that night, and she blames him for ruining her life. I've not been able to see my dad since he was put away, so I don't know his side of the story."

"I'm sorry, Rett, but I read about the accident. He hit them in a crosswalk by running a red light. The papers said that his blood alcohol count was well above point two. How did she figure you were going to join him in jail when you were not even in the same state?" He asked her how she knew that. "I looked it up. When someone is coming to work for me I don't want any surprises. But back to your mother...did you know that there were some issues about her being there or not when the trial was being held?"

"Yes. I guess a neighbor said that he'd seen her or something. And I'm glad to know that you've done your research on me. What else did you find out? I'm sure there is plenty." He watched her take out a pad of paper. Her neat handwriting was on several pages of it, he could see. "You've been very thorough."

"I have been. And what the papers didn't tell me, Danburn did. He told me about how you two were friends." She looked down at her notes. "Your mother tried to have you come home right after the trial, I was told. She said that she needed you there. Also, there was some speculation that she was in the car as well, but neighbors said they'd seen her about an hour before at the house, like you said. Your mom stated your father was driving too fast, as he usually did, and she had stayed home after an argument. But lately she's been saying that she convinced your dad to say he was driving so he would take the blame away from you. That way you could get your career on track. She's a bitch, did you know that?"

"Yes. I've not heard about her turning her story to incriminate me. It sounds like something she'd do, however. And what the paper might not tell you also is that when I was grieving for my dad, she tried to get my license revoked. She wanted me to come home and finance her way of life as my dad had. As it is now, I'm sending her more money than I can afford each month so that she can pay bills and whatnot. My dad had a good job and made great money, and my mom liked things that way. But my dad...well, apparently he's happy being in prison."

"So I heard. He also misses you." Rett told her that wasn't right. According to his mom, he never wanted to see him again. Then he asked her when she'd talked to him. "This morning. That's why Danburn called you. Your dad reached out to him and asked if he could please help you out. He thinks your mother is going to harm you."

"She has." Rett couldn't take much of talking about his mom, so he changed the subject. He asked her about their marriage, the castle, and a great many other mundane things. He was happy when she didn't bring his mom or dad up again.

And now here he sat, in a castle, trying to figure out how this was going to work for them all. He wanted to do this, very much so. But as he'd told Danburn and his wife several times, he didn't have the experience that was needed to run a household's money like they had. Both of them had told him he'd be fine. He certainly hoped so.

Rett had three emails from his old firm, one from his dad, which really surprised him, and another from his mother. He figured he'd get the bad news over first. So he opened the one from his mother, marked *urgent*. With her, everything was urgent.

Dear ungrateful son. He had to laugh at that one. She was forever coming up with ways to put him in his place. He'd yet to figure out what he was ungrateful about, but he read on. *I heard from your former boss yesterday. He told me that you've quit your job and you're not living in that place you were before. I've no idea how he might have come to this information when you'd not told me. So I had to check it out for myself, thinking that no son of mine would just up and leave without telling his dear mother. But I did find that not only had you left, but your place has been rented again. Just how long will you be gone, and how long before you're employed again? I need that money that you send me monthly, Everette. Just because you've lost your mind, if you ever had one, there is no reason that I should have to go without.*

There was no ending to the letter, just her wanting his money. Money that he had to work very hard for. So, feeling pretty good about himself and his new life, he decided to write her back. Normally, he'd just call, but he wanted to say things to her and not have her cut him off, as she was prone to do.

Mother. Yes, I'm so very ungrateful. I moved out of my house only three days ago, but it's nice to know that you cared enough to be curious. Or was it just the money that you're wondering about? Money you think I owe you?

I've come to a lot of decisions of late, especially concerning you and my making sure you have a roof over your head. I've decided that my head needs covering more than yours. You will have to use some of the money you currently have in the bank to cover your monthly expenses, whatever they might be.

That had been a surprise to him. To find out from Danburn

that not only did his mom have money in the bank, but she had a great deal of it. Like nearly a million dollars. And the money he'd been sending her each month, of which he could ill afford, had been paying for small things like tea pots and china cups that she was taking to the backyard and shattering. Just, he supposed, because she could. He continued with his letter, smiling now.

I'm going to visit Dad in a few days as well. He has asked that I come. Imagine my surprise when he told me that he'd been begging for some way to contact me, and you told him that he was dead to me. I told him you'd said the same to me, telling me that since I didn't take the fall for him that he hated me. What a horrific thing to say to a son about his dad.

Rett thought about what else he could tell her. Maybe question her about some things like the money and how she had used his as well. But all he could think about was how his father had sobbed when he'd called him. Cried out how much he'd missed him and wanted to see him. So Rett ended his letter to his mother.

I'm ashamed to call you my mother. I've given this a great deal of thought, talked about your behavior with others, and I'm done with you. You can have the kind of life you want, without me in it. As I said, I'm through. Goodbye, Mother, I'd prefer that you didn't contact me again. Then he signed it Rett, a nickname that she hated as much as she apparently did him.

After that, it was a pleasure to read the mail from his former boss. He was saying that as he'd not given notice that he was no longer entitled to the discounts he had been getting. His three weeks of vacation pay had been forfeited, as he'd thought they would be. And they wanted to remind him he had a gag order in place and wasn't to talk about the firm with anyone. He forwarded it, along with the one that told him he wasn't going to get a nice recommendation from them concerning any job that he applied to, to Danburn.

His dad's letter was both uplifting and sad. Rett really did miss his father, and hated that for the last sixteen years his mother had kept them apart. He finished it up just as his cell phone went off. It was the clinic.

"My name is Casandra Harmon. They call me Cassie here. Like you need to know that. But anyway, there's a gentleman here by the name of Pits, I'm not sure if it's just a nickname or his actual name.... I'm sorry. I'm not doing this well. There is a gentleman here by the name of Pits, and he needs your assistance if you can spare a few minutes. He's having trouble with his checks." He asked Cassie if it was his benefits check. "No. I think it's just with checks in general. I've tried to explain to him that there isn't much we can do if the bank tells him they're not printed right. But he thinks he needs professional help. So do I, but I'm pretty sure that we're not on the same page about that."

Rett laughed. He was sure she'd not meant to say the last part aloud, but he enjoyed it. After he told her that he was on his way, she thanked him. Rett hadn't met the woman as yet, but he knew what she was. Danburn told him that she was Kendrick's assistant as well.

The car that had been purchased for his use was a treat for him. Rett hadn't been able to afford one since he'd been a sixteen-year-old with a piece of shit model that he worked on more than drove. His dad and he had worked on it for a week one summer, and he wasn't sure they'd done it much good. But it had been a great deal of fun for them both, he remembered.

Mr. Pits was waiting at the door for him. Rett had been told there were rooms he could use at the clinic, and led the elderly gentleman to one of those now. The man explained, or tried to, what he needed from him as they walked.

"They said that the lines are wrong." Rett took the checkbook that was shoved at him. "I don't have no lines on them checks, and when I offered to.... There was this one time when I was in a bank and they asked me if I had an account. I asked her on account of what, and she told me to leave. But them lines aren't on there."

Rett had to think before speaking. Sorting out the information was difficult enough without having to deal with the way Mr. Pits smelled. Christ, he'd bet he'd not seen a bar of soap in ten years if not more. Kendrick had told him, several times yesterday, that if they needed to bathe to tell them. He thought it would be hard to do until today.

"How long have you been here in this building?" He told him three days. "And in all that time, you never thought to make use of the shower?"

"I don't have no lines on my —"

"I don't care about the lines right now. I want you to know that I'll help you as best I can, but you need to go and take a shower, use the deodorant that is there for you, as well as the clean clothing. Until you've done that, I can't help you. Actually, I won't help you." The man huffed at him. "You want my help, then you have to help me. Take a bath so that I don't have to be sick while we're in this room together."

"That girl, she told me the same thing. What the hell do I

need a bath for if I only want money?" Rett leaned back in his chair, mostly to distance himself from Mr. Pits. "I don't like you and your orders. I'll do this, but I don't have to like it."

"No, you don't, but as I said, if you want my help, then you have to smell less like a garbage can and more like a human being. A clean one." He told him he wasn't. "What are you then?"

"Alien. Aliens don't take baths like humans do." He wasn't sure if he was to believe him or not, and looked at the doorway when someone cleared their throat. He figured it was the famed Cassie. "She's been telling me all along that I'm just plain human too. Can't convince her otherwise."

"Perhaps if you bathed then we'd both be able to tell." The man huffed again. "Bathe or not, it's up to you. But I'm not going to help you until you do."

When he left with the woman, Rett opened the checkbook. There weren't any lines on the check, which he already knew, but he did call the bank. By the time they'd discussed it, Mr. Pits came back. Not only had Rett straightened things out with the bank, but he also had a better understanding of Mr. Pits. There had been a note on his file to call his doctor, someone at the veterans' office, where Pits was a sometime patient.

He was bipolar. Not only that, but he suffered from major depression, both things that Rett had little to no information on. The doctor said he had medication, his prescriptions were up to date, but he didn't take them like he was supposed to.

The bank person was less than helpful, but Rett thought it was because she was so frustrated with Mr. Pits. She told him that she did try to explain things to him—David, his first name was—but he was too stubborn to listen. Rett wrote himself a note to contact the bank manager and have him talk to his staff about dealing with people. Or he'd have to deal with them in the form of legal action.

"The lines that she was referring to are your balance sheet, not on your checks." He showed him what she'd been trying to explain to the man. "There is just over two thousand dollars in your account. Does that sound right?"

"I have more in my passbook account, but she won't let me touch that." He asked him if it was the same bank. "Yes, sir, but it's not the bank that won't let me touch it, it's my granddaughter. She's staying at my house, not that I invited her in or nothing, but there she is, living it up like the queen of the castle. She's like her momma, a really hard person to like. I'm thinking she is just waiting for me to keel over so she can have it all. I ain't sure why I think that, but my alien friend, he told me she was gonna rob me blind. I like seeing well enough, but I sure could use me some new specs too."

"I can set you up with a doctor for your glasses. But this granddaughter thing, is she really related to you, or your alien friend? Where do you live, Mr. Pits? I can have a talk with her and see what I can work out for you." He told him the address. "Do you plan to go back there this evening? I can go with you if you want."

"Can't. She made it so that I can't even come on the property at all. And she won't let me get my stuff either. She changed the locks on me." Rett felt his body tense up in anger. "I got me nowhere to go but here. Rachel, she's my granddaughter, said that I wasn't gonna tell her what to do. Never could tell her momma a darn thing too. She'd just blow me off like I done never said a word to her. So one day when I was out and

34

about, I come home and my keys won't work. Said I wasn't going to get in until I signed over some paperwork to her. I didn't do that, I can tell you."

"No, and you won't have to. I'll see what I can do about getting your home back. It might be a simple matter of her wanting you to sign her lease or something." Rett asked about Cassie. "She don't live with me, if that's what you're asking. But as sure as I'm standing here, I'd like that. The aliens tell me that I can't be doing anything bad to myself again either. Cassie is in her office."

"You mean you tried to kill yourself?" He nodded and had the saddest expression on his face that Rett had ever seen. "I don't want you to do that either. We'll work something out, but I have to find Cassie."

David put his fingers in his mouth and made the loudest sound he'd ever heard. It was ear piercing. But it had the desired effect. A woman Rett still assumed was Cassie came into the room a few seconds later.

"If you do that again, I'm going to hit you. I've told you several times now that it hurts." David just laughed. "You won't think it's so funny if my dragon wants to eat you alive for it."

Rett stood up when she came further in the room. Christ, she was beautiful. Sexy too, with her shorts and t-shirt on. He swallowed twice before he even thought about speaking. But she didn't seem to have the problems he did…she seemed to speak her mind. When she told him to shut his mouth, he did so with a snap.

~~~

"I don't think this is a good idea." Rett asked her why.

35

Cassie stretched her neck enough to hear it pop and he laughed. He was driving them to the house to see what was going on. He liked David and wanted to help him work this out. "You won't think this is so funny if I have to take a bullet for you. This woman, she means to take that old man for all he has, and we're going to be in her way."

"Probably. Would you really take a bullet for me?" Her growl had him laughing. "Anyway, I have spoken to Mr. Pits's doctor, and he can live on his own so long as he takes his medications. By the way, I think Rachel is keeping them from him by not giving him access to his money."

"He told me once that he had a house but he wasn't able to live in it. He also said right afterwards that aliens were his friends and they told him to come see me. I wasn't sure which to believe. David has some pretty far out there tales." Cassie realized they were driving so slowly that even a couple walking seemed to be outpacing them. "Did you know that the speed limit here is thirty-five, not five?"

"I've not driven in a long time." He glanced at her and she could see fear there. "I'm okay by myself. I don't have to worry about harming anyone, but with a passenger, I get a little terrified of my ability. I just need more practice."

When he pulled over after she asked him if he wanted her to drive, she wondered about the man. Men, in her experience, didn't like women driving them around, especially out where someone could see them. When she got behind the wheel, she decided to have a little fun with him. He needed to branch out, she thought.

By the time they made it to the house, he was green, and holding on to the door handle and the one above it like it was

36

going to save him. Cassie knew that she drove like she had a death wish, but she didn't think it was that bad. He looked at her when she asked him if he was all right.

"No. I'm pretty sure that I won't be ever again, either. Where the hell did you learn to take a corner like that? Drag racing 101?" She laughed. He was so serious all the time. "Did you know that when the light turns yellow, you're to slow down to stop, not race through it like you're going to try and beat it? It's there for your safety."

"I think I might have read that somewhere." He growled and her body warmed up for some reason. "You can drive on the way back. At least we got here today and not next week."

She was grinning as they made their way to the house. She'd not had this much fun in a good long time. Just as she was going to tell him that, she heard the door open and the smell of gunpowder. Cassie let her dragon take her just as shots were fired.

Her dragon knew just what to do. As Rett fell to the ground, blood spreading across his chest, she called to Danburn and told him what was going on. She felt the connection strong enough to know that he was afraid for them, but was coming.

The woman fired at her. It didn't harm her of course; her body was made of thick scales like armor. But when she aimed the gun at Rett again, Cassie did the only thing she could and blew a white hot flame to stop her. The house caught just as the woman did, but Cassie had more concerns than a fool with a gun coming up against a dragon.

As she landed near Rett, her body shielding him from any more harm, her dragon looked around. It was chancy becoming her other self in the open like this, but she knew that had she not, things might have been much worse. She rolled Rett over when she took her body back.

"I'm going to die." She didn't tell him that she thought so as well. "I'm so sorry I made fun of your driving. It wasn't that bad."

"It was too. Now hush while I have a look." He moaned when she tore his shirt open. Blood was running down his belly and pooling in his navel. Cassie knew that he was only moments from bleeding out. "Do you trust me?"

"I do. I don't know why. I think you're a lunatic, but I trust you." He grinned, and as it faded out, she could hear his heart slowing. "Tell Danburn that he's the best friend I ever had."

"Tell him yourself, jackass."

Letting her monster take her just a little, she ran her tongue over the wound. The bullets, three of them, came out of his chest. Opening her arm up just above the elbow, she put the wound over his mouth. It would either kill him or help, she wasn't sure which. But she moaned when he licked her skin. "Stop playing around and drink. I don't have time for you to be all sexy on me."

His laughter made her think he was delirious, but she never stopped telling him to drink. As soon as Danburn arrived, he called the police. The woman was dead, of course, and the house was burned pretty badly too. There had been no hope for it. It was her or them, and Cassie thought she'd made the right choice.

CHAPTER 3

Rett tried to move but he felt heavy, weighted down. Even lifting his arm was too much and he let it flop back to his side. The laughter nearby had him opening his eyes to see what the fuck Danburn was doing in his home. Then what had happened hit him.

"Don't move." He stopped struggling against the weight, whatever it was. "You have a couple of bruises that are going to hurt you for some time. Also, a lot of blood loss. I'm not sure how bad that is, but let's just say you bled out pretty good before she helped you."

"That woman, David's granddaughter, she shot me." Danburn must have moved closer, because he could see him now. "Cassie…is she all right? By the way, don't ever ride with her. She'll kill you. Perhaps you can get her in some driving school. I think it would benefit the world in general if you did."

"She's in the other room. I had to make her go lie down for a little while. What do you remember after you were shot?" He tried to think, but his head was all fuzzy. Images were blurred. "Rett, whatever it was, tell me."

"Cassie is a dragon." He said that was right. "She...I think she changed into her other half and...I think she gave me her blood. I was shot. I thought I was going to die. I'm pretty sure Cassie thought so as well. I don't know if that's right or not, but I think I saw it on her face."

"That's correct, she did. And yes, she give you her blood. A great deal of it, as a matter of fact." Rett asked him if that was important. "I think so, but I don't know what you'll think. There are only a very few humans that can take dragon blood and it not kill them. One is someone who has just a little dragon DNA in their body to tolerate it. The second type is a woman in labor. I'm not sure why that works, but dragon's blood can lessen the labor time as well as take away some of the pain. I've never had the occasion to—"

"What are you trying so hard not to tell me?" Danburn laughed. "If I thought I could, I'd get up and kick your ass right now."

"Nah, you can't do that. I'm your lord and master." Rett just stared at him. "Okay, the third type is a mate. A mate, of either sex, can save their other half by giving them blood. I didn't know this one, Mom told me when we brought you here. Cassie didn't either, apparently, or I'm pretty sure she wouldn't have bothered with you."

"Well that's...harsh. But I don't understand." Danburn said he would explain again. "No. I mean, mates? I'm not sure about that part. I understand the meaning, but not what that has to do with me and her."

"Cassie is your mate. And you're hers. Welcome to the family." Rett sat up then, his body getting stronger by the minute. Or it was fueled with anger, he wasn't sure. "She

EVERETTE

wasn't sure if her blood would save you or not, but she had
to try. Mom asked her all kinds of questions when we got you
settled, and then she got out the big book."

"You have a big book of dragon stuff?" Danburn said
it wasn't really big, but that's what he'd called it as a child.
"I could easily shoot you right now. What the fuck are you
talking about?"

"Cassie gave you her blood. And in doing so, sealed the
deal, so to speak, about the two of you. You're her other half,
like Kendrick is to me. Mates. I guess you could call it husband
and wife, but this is much stronger than that. You also have
all the traits she does. We think." He asked what that meant.
"Well, you'd have to let me cut you, but I'm pretty sure that
you're an immortal. Nothing can harm you. Well, some things
can, but you have all her power, magic, and immortality. You
can't shift, but you can do just about everything else she can."

Rett asked him to slow down, he needed to think. "When
we got there, we were talking about...her driving is scary.
Anyway, I was walking to the house, just kidding around,
and suddenly I felt like someone had stabbed me in the chest."
Danburn said that was when he'd been shot. "She shifted.
Cassie turned into a dragon and...and I think she sprayed her
fire over the house. And the woman there."

"Yes. But if anyone asks, when you arrived the house was
already engulfed in flames. You were knocked out by flying
debris." Rett looked at Danburn when he spoke again. "Cassie
saved your life, Rett. And in doing so, she found her mate."

Rett wasn't sure how long he just laid there after Danburn
left. He had been deep in thought, trying his best to work out
whatever the hell had happened. When he looked up, he

saw that Kendrick had taken the place of Danburn and was smiling at him.

"You hungry?" He said that he didn't think so. "Good answer. At least you're not saying no. I have no idea why, but they seem to think it's really important that you eat soon. Can I have someone bring you at least a smoothie or anything?"

"Not yet." He looked around. "Where is Cassie? She's not in trouble is she? I mean, I know that she killed that woman, but I don't think she was going to just fire a warning shot at us and be done with it." Kendrick said that Cassie was still resting. "Is she all right? I mean, Danburn said she was lying down earlier."

"I guess it takes a lot out of a dragon to give someone blood. Not to mention, she brought you back here too. Not as her dragon, but one of her powers is the ability to move really fast. Danburn has a few too, he told me, but not that one." Rett knew she was stalling, but with Kendrick, he decided to let her tell him something in her own way. "Saving you really hurt her dragon. I don't think…this is just me, but I feel she doesn't really care if she makes it or not."

"You mean she wants to die?" Kendrick shrugged. "Tell me what you know, please? I'm much better now that I've had time to digest this all. Danburn said she was my mate and that there were only a few humans that could take the blood of one of their kind. I got that part. What I don't understand, and you might not either, is how did her giving me blood make us mates?"

"It didn't." He looked at the doorway when Cassie spoke. She looked like hell and he told her so. "Thank you so much. The next time I nearly kill myself trying to save your ass, I'll remember to do my hair and nails first."

"When you paint them, are your dragons' nails painted as well?" He felt his entire body heat up with embarrassment. "I have no idea where that thought came from. It just...poof, it was there. I'm so sorry."

Kendrick was still laughing when she left. Something about making arrangements for dinner. Rett asked Cassie to have a seat and she did. When she seemed to settle, he asked her if she was all right.

"Yes. Tired, but all right. How are you?" He told her he felt pretty good. "I'm glad. I didn't even think when my dragon took me. That's only happened a couple of times, where my dragon will just come out to save my ass."

"I'm very glad that she did this time." Cassie yawned and he did too. "Come here and lie down. We can talk about anything you want, but I'd like for you to rest."

"I'm all right." When she yawned a fourth time, he moved the blankets over and asked her to please join him. "I hurt with exhaustion, Rett. I'm so sorry about the other thing."

"We'll figure something out." She finally joined him on the bed. Rett scooted down on his bed and pulled her body to his. She was very warm, and he asked her if she was fevered.

"I'm a dragon, dork. We're hot."

Laughing a little, he snuggled closer to her. It wasn't until he yawned for the fourth or fifth time that he realized how tired he was as well. Closing his eyes, he felt sleep drag him under, and his last thoughts were that Cassie was holding him and she'd saved his life.

~~~

Cassie wasn't sure where she was for a moment, but she

was comfortable. Rolling to her back, she opened her eyes and looked up at the man leaning over her. Rett. Her mate. Touching her fingers to his cheek, she felt the weight of several worlds lift from her shoulders when he smiled at her.

"You talk in your sleep." She nodded. Cassie had been told that before. "Am I supposed to be jealous of someone called Banger?"

"My cat. He hated me as much as I loved him. But like a lot of things do when you can outlive them, he passed away and left me all alone. I buried him in the family cemetery so that I can visit when I want." He nodded. "You're not at all what I expected. If I ever thought to find a mate. There aren't too many of us left. Dragons, I mean. A few, but not like there used to be."

"I'm not sure what to expect from you, if anything. I never thought I'd find the right woman either." He leaned down and kissed her. It was quick and warm. "Does it work this way? I mean, feeling like you've just been given a great gift in having someone in your life? I mean, this fast?"

"I don't know. I didn't have all that good of role models for wedded bliss. My parents were.... My mom was a wonderful person, but she died when I was just a child. She got an infection of some kind and didn't respond well to medications. Not that there were many around for her, but my dad...he said she died peacefully." He nodded. "My dad is a bastard and an abusive person. He was tolerable when I was younger and my mom was around, but I've since come to realize that he wasn't a good man to her either. I don't much care for him or how he treats me. Are you going to kiss me again?"

"Yes. In a moment." She reached up and curled her hand around his neck. "Are you going to always be this greedy?"

"Yes." She felt his weight on her, his body moving over hers as she deepened the kiss. He was firm in all the right places. Soft in others. As his hands roamed over her, all Cassie could think about was how much she wanted him to take her, make love to her.

Her breasts were bared to him. As he suckled at the tip of one, pulling her hard nipple into his mouth, Cassie reached down and cupped his cock in her hand. When he moaned, she could feel it all over her body.

Cassie liked sex all right. Usually she was left sort of disappointed, but she'd always figured that was because of her, not her partner. But this man, even by him just touching her, she knew she was going to enjoy this like she had nothing else.

He moved off her and stood by the side of the bed. Sitting up, she reached for him and he told her to wait. He wanted to see her first. She warmed more, her dragon moving over her body.

"Take off your clothes. Start with your shirt." He'd already torn it, but she pulled it over her head and let it drop to the floor. Her bra was next. He moaned loudly, the sound of it like warm butter being spread over hot biscuits. "Your breasts are the most beautiful I've ever seen. And your nipples taste like gumdrops."

"Let me see your cock, Rett. It's all I can think of. I know that you're thick, but I want to see it." He nodded and reached to the pants that Danburn had put on him when he'd been hurt. "All I can think about is sucking you into my mouth.

45

Having you come down my throat over and over."

"Christ, woman, are you trying to kill me?" He freed his cock and wrapped his hand around himself. Cassie licked the tip, just enough to taste the cum that was streaming from the tiny hole there. "Strip, baby. I need to fuck you."

She stood up then, making short work of her clothing. When he reached for her, wrapping his arm around her waist and pulling her flush to his body, she felt her pussy gush hotly. And as he leaned down and took her breast, all of it, in his mouth, she cried out when he bit down on her.

He rocked into her. Not entering her, not yet, but his cock was at her pussy and touching off all kinds of sensations within her. Cassie could have easily come then, just let her body have its release as he played with her. Every place his fingers touched it was like a brand on her skin. Each breath he took was like a lick of flames over her. Cassie was needy, her body simmering for his.

"Come for me."

Like she'd been primed for it, her body let go. She screamed out her release, and when his cock rolled over her clit twice more, she came a second time. Her body was hot for his. The need for him to take her was there, but he wasn't finished just yet. Turning her around, Rett had her lean over as he went to his knees. He spread her legs wider as he filled her with his fingers.

His mouth was all over her. Her legs, her ass. He licked the back of her knees, his fingers filled her pussy. Every time she thought she was going to come, he'd move again. Her body was burning up with need and he was making her crazy.

"Please, Rett, I need you." He told her she was in too

much of a hurry. "Please, I beg of you. Fuck me."

She felt his movements, knew when he was standing behind her. And when she felt his cock at her entrance again, she rolled her hips backward, trying her best to get him to fill her. When he did move forward, his cock filling her at last, she knew a new kind of torture.

He was thicker than she'd imagined. Fuller too. As he moved in and out of her, slowly like he was bent on killing her, she felt his balls as they touched her backside. She needed not just to come, but all of it, and he was denying her that.

As he moved into her as slowly as he could, Cassie tried to get him to hurry, to finish her, even going so far as to reach between her legs and touch him. Nothing was working. He was on a mission, it seemed, to make her suffer greatly.

"Please?" He laughed, a gentle sort of sound that didn't upset her but made her smile in return. "I want you to know that when I have my way with you, I'm going to make you suffer in ways you cannot imagine."

"I don't think you can do that." He slammed deep, taking her breath away with it. "If I fuck you hard, will you scream out my name? Or will you perhaps come so hard that you faint on me?"

"Fuck me. Now, Rett, fuck me." He pounded her. His hands at her hips held her steady as his cock felt like a jackhammer inside of her. "Yes, more. I need more."

He took her to the bed, his cock deep inside, and she screamed when he grabbed a handful of her hair and lifted her up. His command to come, to let go, had her body pausing, her heart stopping. Then she came.

Nothing could have prepared her for the feeling. And she

did feel, everywhere. Cassie came, hard, long, and tightly. When she screamed out her release a second time, his name was there for him to hear, but she was coming a third, then a fourth as he slammed his cock deeper, harder as his hand dug into her flesh. The world around her narrowed, her heart stopped beating all together, and she let the darkness just take her under.

When she woke she was alone in the bed. The room was dark, but with her advanced eyesight, she was able to see that she was also the only one in the room too. Getting up, wrapping the sheet around her, she looked in the bathroom and found him in the tub, water up to his chin.

"Hey there. I needed to try and work out some of this soreness. I hate baths normally, but I was aching a little." She let the towel drop. "You do that and we'll mess up this very lovely bathroom."

She told him she didn't care. "This room, like the others in the house, is made of stone from the mountain, did you know that?" He said that he didn't. "The water, too, comes from the earth, and is a constant flow that is warmer than a bath would be. The entire place is filled with little touches that the earth has given Danburn. Do you like it?"

"Yes, I really do. But I did wonder why it was just full of water when I came in here. Are you going to join me or just give a history on the house?" She did join him, but continued with what she knew about the house.

"Danburn built this place with his magic. He asked the earth for a place to hold his family and she helped him with it. The area around here was barren when he started this." She took the small sponge from him and started washing his body. "The ring that Kendrick wears is from the earth as well. Apparently, the lady earth was holding it for her until Kendrick came to be with him."

"He told me once that he was very old. I'm assuming that you are as well." She nodded, not sure if he was ready to know her age. "Don't tell me. I'm still slightly overwhelmed by this whole thing. I loved your dragon, by the way. What I got to see of her."

"She's not like Danburn's. I mean, she's a dragon, but his is a warrior kind. I'm sort of just a rider. The kind that warriors, and humans, would ride into battle. My mom was one as well, but she had a great deal of magic that kept her from having to serve that way." She moved so that her back was to his chest, her legs between his. As he smoothed his hands over her head and shoulders, she began to relax again. "When I was younger and my mother still alive, I saw her flying. It wasn't uncommon to see dragons in the sky then, but it was for me to see my mom. She was beautiful. Her wings were light like the sky, her body moved like she owned the currents that kept her up. And when she landed before me, I thought of all the others that I'd seen in my life and thought my mother the most beautiful. I still do, but it was then that I realized that she was special."

"Because she was your mom?" She turned and looked at him. How did she explain to him how very special they both were, her and her mom? "What is it? You can tell me anything."

"Okay, but it's all right if you get a little weirded out. Here goes…I'm descended from a long line of magical dragons. The women in our family aren't like most. We can do things as our dragons that no one, regardless the age, ever achieves. It gets stronger, this magic, and when I pass it on to my children, they'll be able to do things that I can't." He nodded, not really understanding her, she could tell. "Watch."

Putting her hand just above the water, she called to it. As it started to rise from the tub, she raised her hand higher and the water followed. Spreading her fingers out, the water, now under her command, started to spread out as well, spraying a gentle rain-like spray over them both.

When he didn't comment, she thought perhaps he was going to be all right with this. Most men, in her experience, weren't. Even her father, who knew firsthand what it was like to live with someone magical, had been terrified of her mom's.

"I can do the same with wind. For a fire breathing dragon to have control over the elements is very rare and slightly dangerous. However, the women in my family have been able to do it since birth." He asked her if she could make it do anything else. "Yes. I can make it narrow down to a point, aim it at things, and hit it. Once when I was showing off to some guy, I was at a fair and he was trying to win me a bear or something. Anyway, I took aim with one of the guns that spray water and hit the target every time."

"I bet he just loved you showing him up." She laughed. "Okay, so you have power over the elements. What else is there? I know there's more."

"Yes." He stood up when she asked him to. "Don't freak out. I mean, if you do, I won't blame you, but please, just try and not scream."

"All right. But I want you to know that I do freak out easily, especially lately." She called her dragon and asked her to show her mate. "Holy fucking Christ, Cassie."

Cassie knew what he was seeing...six smaller dragons that looked exactly like her and herself. While they were independent of her, she could control their movements as well as their flight. But when necessary they could branch off from her and go up to a hundred miles away to help.

She flew to the countertop and they followed her. Sitting down, she called them and they formed around her. When she took her body back, she picked up the sheet and held it in front of her, waiting for his reaction.

"I don't know...you can separate into smaller versions of yourself? I mean, they sort of just come off you, right?" She nodded. "Do you command them or do they, I don't know, work independently of you?"

"I can control them, but I don't have to. They have thoughts, minds of their own. I can call them to me, but they also can go where needed. I can only separate so that there are six. I'm not sure why, but that's as far as I can go. My mom and grandmother could do more, but I think it was because they were a great deal older than me." He nodded. "Are you all right?"

"I am. I'm not sure how sane I'm feeling right now, but I'm all right. Can I ask questions? I mean, it won't upset you, will it?" She told him to go ahead. But she was feeling out of her element with him just standing there naked. "Can you do that as a human? I mean, become more?"

He reached for a towel and wrapped it around his hips. She wasn't sure that was any better. It felt like he'd drawn a curtain between them. She fought hard to keep the tears she could feel from falling. It felt as if he was rejecting her. Cassie didn't know why, but that was how she was feeling.

"No, just as a dragon. And they can only be dragons, not humans. I should go now." He asked her why. "I don't know. I kind of feel like I'm doing something wrong."

"You're not. I'm…this is all new to me. All of this. Dragons and mates. I should be dead right now, but you saved me. Just give me a few minutes to try and process this, all right?" She nodded, but he came to her. "Please don't cry. It's all my fault, and I'm so sorry."

"I just wanted to impress you." He laughed. "It's not funny. Do you have any idea how hard this has been for me to show you?"

"Yes, I believe that I do. But you have to understand how hard this is for me too. I've never dealt with anything like this, ever. You've had your entire life, a lot more time than I can even imagine having. You have to listen to me, Cassie. Everything you do? Every time you shift or do these things? It's like my entire world has gone off the deep end." She looked at him. "I'm trying my best not to freak out like you asked me not to. I'm being calm, cool, and collected. But inside? I'm a mess. I want you to tell me what else it is you can do because of what you are, but slowly. Maybe one thing a day."

"All right." Rett held her in his arms, and she felt better. Not great, but better. "I can change you into a worm if you want."

She laughed so hard at the expression on his face that she had to hold onto the counter. He kept telling her she wasn't right, that she was mean. And the more he called her names, the harder she laughed. Finally, when she could no longer support herself, she sat on the counter and grinned at him.

"You have a mean streak in you." She nodded. "I think I might like spending the rest of my days with you."

"I know you said one thing at a time, but there is something important you should be aware of. You're an immortal." He told her she was funny. "I'm not kidding about this. You're going to live as long as you want. And you'll heal faster and not get sick again either. It was part of what you got when you took my blood into your body. It not just healed you, but made you...I guess more."

"I thought Danburn was kidding." She shook her head. "Really? Forever? I mean, your mother passed away. I know that Danburn's father did as well. How did that happen if he was an immortal?"

"I don't know about his dad, but my mom died when she was sick. I've always thought it was because she'd gotten something with a bit of iron in it and no one thought to look for it. Iron will harm if not kill most supernaturals." Rett moved to the bedroom with her as she continued. "I don't remember the year, but we were hunted, as I told you, and they figured out somehow that it, in any shape, can poison our blood. Even Danburn has to be careful of it. You should ask him about his dad. He might have died the same way."

Cassie told him about her life, growing up during a time when she was hunted by men with pitchforks and swords. He told her of his mom and what sort of person she was. They had dinner with Danburn and Kendrick, where Danburn told them how his dad had died, and when his mom joined them, she told stories of her own childhood. Cassie thought it was the most enjoyable time she'd had in a long while.

Chapter 4

Elba Welsh let the phone ring six times, then hung up when the mechanical voice told her that voice mail wasn't set up for this number. Everette was going to hear about this as soon as she spoke to him. As she settled back down on her chair, Elba let out a long breath. The boy was going to have to reconsider his way of thinking, and soon.

"And he's not going to see his father either. I don't care how old he is, I'm still the boss. And he had better start remembering that too. The nerve of that boy. To think that I allowed him to live, and he treats me this way." She wondered when he got this notion in his head that he could just tell her to back off. "I'll show you what I do when someone upsets me. I make them understand that I'm the one with all the answers."

Elba hated her husband. Didn't care for his son either. But as the wife and mother, she knew she'd have to endure them a little longer. Neither had any idea how much she suffered because of them. She wasn't one to complain, really, but she did let them know when they messed up her plans. And both of them were doing just that. Elba was going to have to do something drastic if they didn't straighten up, and soon. She glanced at the email that had arrived two days ago from the department of corrections.

Her husband was up for parole. Not exactly, she supposed, but release. The email she'd gotten from his attorney said that there was new evidence brought forward, and she'd have to appear in court soon. Nine days until she had to go through all this again with her husband. A little over a week until she would be sitting in a courtroom filled with people she didn't like any more than she did her family, and going over the same things over and over. He'd better not be trying to change his story. She'd have to talk with him about that soon.

George, Everette's father, had been gone from her life nearly sixteen years. And to have him return now, after she'd gotten things just the way she wanted, was just not right. The staff, the few she had working for her, knew only to answer to her. It was the way she wanted it, not having a husband around to try and tell them differently.

Then there was Everette. He'd better not think that he was off the hook either. And the money he was sending each month was going to continue as well. Not that she needed it, but there was a point to this, and he was certainly going to do as she said. She wondered where he'd gotten the gumption to think he could just do as he wanted. As much as the vulgarity of the term bothered her, she thought that he'd gotten some balls.

"Well, he's going to have to give them to me too. I'll not have him treating me this way." She sat higher on her chair, trying to make herself look slimmer. Elba worked hard at making her body appear younger than it was. Vanity was the one vice that she had, she knew this, but she didn't want to look or act like an old woman, and it cost her dearly each month to keep her appearances perfect.

Elba didn't need the money. She just didn't want Everette to have it. When he was broke and not making ends meet, she felt he was getting just what he deserved for being born and messing up her life.

It was a small price to pay for all the things she'd had to do to bring him into this world. Besides, it gave her a small bit of joy to find a very expensive piece of history and take it in the backyard and destroy it. The ground behind her roses was littered with brightly colored slivers of glass and stoneware from the tea sets she had shipped to her. And for hours after taking a hammer to them, she felt positively wonderful.

Long ago when she'd found out she was carrying her husband's child, she didn't know anything about abortions or doctors who did things like that. Had she, there wouldn't have been this albatross hanging around her neck and she could be whatever she wanted. Not that she didn't now, but having a child had ruined her body, and for that alone she could never forgive him.

"Bastard. And the pain I endured to bring him into this world makes me wish I'd had the nerve to fall down a few more times. He's going to have to work very hard for me to.... Well, I won't forgive him, but I will make him suffer a bit more from now on." She reached for the little weights she'd picked up when she'd been visiting. Although that really wasn't what she'd been doing.

The liposuction on her legs had been painful, but well worth it. She had the legs of a twenty-year-old. Last year she'd had her belly and arms done. Her arms were lovely, the fat that hung under them was gone. But she'd never been satisfied with her belly. She was positive the man had done nothing more than hurt her. Elba had made sure he paid for that mistake too.

Elba trusted no one with any sort of knowledge about herself, not on a personal level. Of course, everyone knew about her husband and his murderous ways. She had liked the way the papers and others had given her sympathy for a time.

If George thought she was going to take him back after all this, then he was even more stupid than his son. She didn't even want him living in her town, much less her home. He needed to find himself other means of support. Elba wasn't going to help him get his life together. And there was no way she'd let him touch her. When they were first married, he used to like hugging and holding her hand. Well, that was finished too. Her body was her own, and he'd have to get used to that.

Not that he did that much before he'd left anyway. She could not stand sex and had told him that every day. It was messy and very nasty as far as she was concerned. And to have him touch her while she was naked had made her positively ill. He was probably sleeping with other inmates anyway. That's all they did in prison, she knew...have sex with one another.

Elba lifted the small weights twelve times and then put them down. In an hour she'd do it again. She was going to shed these extra pounds even if she had to go and convince that doctor again, with her gun this time, that he needed to simply cut it from her body. She would not be one of those old fat women that could only wear workout pants when they went out. And those old people shoes? There wasn't any way she'd be caught dead in those either.

She looked down at her ankle. Yesterday she'd taken a hard tumble off her heels and had really hurt herself. Then she'd ended up in the emergency room because of the overwhelming pain. Elba had wanted to slap the doctor when he'd dared to tell her that she needed to wear more conventional shoes at her age. And had even suggested that she try and walk in more smooth places. The cane he'd given her gave her a few ideas on other uses for it, so that she kept. It might come in handy, she thought, when dealing with her son and husband.

"Just how old did he think I was, I'd like to know?" She huffed and decided that she would call the hospital in the morning and have that man fired and her records destroyed. She did not know why they had her age on file, but that was going to go too. "I do not like to be reminded of things better left unsaid."

Picking up the phone again, she called her son. She'd made a note of not just the time that she made the call, but how many times it rang without being answered. She knew that he was ignoring her. After that email he'd sent, he had to know she was going to be upset with him. But this time there was a message, or at least it didn't tell her that no box had been set up as yet.

"About time you got off your lazy bottom and did this. Stupid boy probably had to have help with it first." She listened to the message left for callers. Elba disconnected then called right back. There wasn't any way he'd left a message like that.

"Mother, stop calling this number. I am not, under any circumstances, going to speak to you. You're wasting your time. Don't bother leaving a message, I won't return any calls. As I have said, I'm done with you."

"Of all the nerve of that boy. Well, we'll just see about that, won't we?" She dialed the number a total of nineteen more times, each time leaving the same message. "Ungrateful child."

When she felt that she'd done her duty, she got up and hobbled to her bedroom. It was time to show that little bastard she was still his mother no matter what he said or did to her. And when she was finished with him, she was going to make sure that his father stayed right where he was too. Elba would not have her entire life in an upheaval just because no one respected her the way they should.

Elba made note of every penny she had to spend to take care of this. Everette was going to reimburse her no matter what he thought about sending her money. There was the cab ride to the airport, and her ticket. She even charged him tips, even though she would never leave any for someone. It was her feeling that if you couldn't find a job that paid you well enough, then you didn't deserve her hard earned money. Finally, she was ready to board.

She called her son once more. "I'm coming to bring you to heel, you thankless boy. And when I get there, you had better have your wallet out. This is costing me a great deal to make sure you know who is boss. And you're also going to reimburse me for the detective I had to hire to find your ungrateful ass."

The flight to where he was irritated her to no end. She had

to share her seating with some woman who was constantly talking to anyone that would listen. Elba thought about kicking or even slapping her, but she was sure that instead of putting the woman somewhere else, like off the plane, she'd be the one that was punished. There was nothing but stupid people everywhere.

By the time she landed, none too soon as far as she was concerned, Elba had a list of things she was going to say to her son. Another had been started on things that her husband was going to say and do, as well to make sure that he stayed where he was. She had no idea why they were doing this to her, but she was going to take matters into her own hands and finish it. The men in her life would rue the day that they thought they could treat her with anything less than perfection.

~~~

Danburn had never had the pleasure of meeting Rett's parents. Not until recently anyway. But since then, he'd gone to talk to his father twice, and he knew that Rett had gone a few times as well. He was a good man who was very proud of his only son, he'd just been given a shitty deal.

And today, Danburn was going to meet Rett's mother, a person he thought might cause more trouble than she was worth. He had volunteered to pick her up at the airport, as Rett was interviewing for the position of mayor, a job that Danburn thought he was well suited for. However, the conversation he'd had before leaving him at the courthouse made him think that Rett didn't think he could do much of anything. And that, Danburn thought, was because of his mother.

"You can do this." Rett had shaken his head as soon as Danburn had said what he needed him for. "You can. You're perfect for the job. It's what you were born to do."

"I'm barely an attorney, Danburn. I'm sure that you have the wrong person in mind for this. I can't do it." Danburn hated to do it, but he reminded him of the promise he'd made all those years ago. "You can't be serious. You bring that up now? And you want me to be mayor? I mean, Christ. I need to get my life together first."

"Your life is just fine now that you're here. You have friends around you all the time. A lovely dragon in your corner, and Kendrick said if you didn't at least try for this, she was going to kick your ass." Rett looked up at him. "You're afraid of her too, aren't you?"

"Yes. She's scary. When you look at her, you think, oh what a lovely little thing. She'd not hurt a fly. Then she goes into this...I don't know, protective mode, and you want to run. What is she going to do when she has children? I'd hate to be around when someone tries to hurt one of them. Wait, she'll raise the children to be hellions just like her. No, I don't want her pissed off." He shivered. "Do you really think she'd hurt me?"

"Yes." Rett glared and Danburn had laughed. Actually, he still did when he thought of the look on his face. Then he'd gotten the message from Rett's mother.

She wasn't just a mean person, but also vindictive, harsh, rude, and cheap. Not to say she didn't have money for things, but for whatever reason, she didn't use hers when she could bully someone else into using theirs. She had a great deal of it too, but she was still cheap. And he didn't understand that part of her façade.

Danburn knew for a fact that she went to pantries every

time they were giving away food or free meals. She also took advantage of clothing giveaways at the local churches. Then instead of wearing any, she would put them on one of those selling places on the Internet. He'd heard from the neighbors she had a stockpile of food in her pantry, more than a single person could eat in a year.

Her lawn was mowed by the county, trees trimmed the same way. When he'd asked why they were doing it, the officer at the county seat had told him it was easier to just do as she told them and not have to put up a fight. She also demanded that her house be painted twice a year, by the same people who did her yardwork. Danburn could not wait to put this woman in her place, once and for all.

And for some reason she hated Rett and his father. Made no bones whatsoever about how she loathed them and wished they were not around. Elba was a person used to getting her own way all the time, and damn the people who tried to do things differently. It was no wonder that Rett had left her, Danburn thought. She was a first-class bitch.

Danburn looked over at Kendrick and smiled. She was all fired up right now, and he was sort of terrified and excited to see her in defense of Rett. Cassie was with them, but at the moment she was pacing, something he realized that Rett did as well when he was nervous or working out a problem. Which the only one that Danburn could see with this was where to bury the old woman's body.

"Her plane just landed." Danburn stood up as he spoke. Noah asked if he wanted him to get her luggage. "Yes. Thank you. But don't put it in the car just yet. Maybe she'll do us all a favor and leave again."

"It's doubtful. Women like her think they are always correct. Much like a certain gentleman I know." As he walked away, Danburn laughed. Noah was getting more and more sly every day. He had a feeling he was picking it up from Kendrick.

Cassie was ahead of them as they made their way to the gate, which was fine by him. Elba Welsh was in for a rude awakening if she thought she could push Rett's mate around. But he had taken the time to ask her not to murder the woman with witnesses.

"I don't think anyone would care." He said he didn't either, but it would be messy. "I suppose. But I could pay for it. I really wouldn't mind, just so you know. Oh, and I talked to David, the homeless guy at the shelter? He's taking his meds and doing very well. I thank you for getting him live-in help. And he is really happy with the redo on his house."

The elderly man had not shed one tear for his granddaughter when he'd been told of her demise. While he understood why, it didn't make it any less sad that he was glad to be done with her. There had been no mention of Rett being hurt either. It was just a simple fire as far as he had been made aware of.

David had been a little upset about the house, but Danburn had told him that there was insurance for such things and that it was being repaired. The house fire, which was what David had been told happened, took her life, but he said it was her own fault for kicking him to the curb like an old worn out shoe.

Danburn knew who Elba was the moment she disembarked from the plane. There was no doubt in his mind she was going to be trouble. It looked like she was spoiling for a fight from the get go. Cassie, he had to give her credit, walked right up to the woman and smiled, putting out her hand in the process. Elba looked like she wanted to bite it off rather than take it in friendship.

"I'm Cassie Harmon, soon to be Welsh. I guess we'll be related." Elba just stared at her. "I'd really hate for us to get off on the wrong foot. Why don't you just nod and say you're glad to meet me?"

"But I'm not. And I have no idea why you think you're going to be changing your name to Welsh. You're not marrying my son, so long as I have breath in my body." He thought Cassie said that could be arranged too, but wasn't sure. Danburn cleared his throat, which had Elba looking at him. "Who are you? And where is that ungrateful son of mine? I told him to be here, and he'd better be."

"He's not coming. We're taking you to your hotel. Then you can—"

"I will not be riding anywhere with you. You're a stranger to me. What do you think I am, easy?" Danburn started to speak, to tell her exactly what he thought she was, but Kendrick poked him in the ribs. "What is the meaning of this? Where is Everette?"

"He's working." Elba huffed and told him that was doubtful. "Not only is he working, but he might be the new mayor of our town. Quite a coup for him, don't you think?"

"No, I do not. He isn't smart enough for such a position. Why, he can't even hold down a decent job, the moron. I want you to call right now and have him come here." She looked around and then glared at him. "What is that man doing with my luggage? I never gave him permission to touch—"

"Shut up." Everyone turned to Cassie when she spoke. "Christ, you do go on, don't you? Now, let's get a few things straight right now, you old biddy. Rett is at an interview and won't be coming to get you. You either come with us, right now, or spend whatever time you wish in this airport. I, for one, would love it if you just got your harpy ass back on that thing and never returned, but you came here for some reason that only you can understand. So, you might as well have your say and get it over with. Then we can get on with our lives without you there constantly going on about shit that doesn't concern you. What's it going to be?"

"You will not speak to me in such a manner. I am your elder, and demand that you respect my position as Everette's mother." Cassie just laughed. "You're very disrespectful. I don't like you. And if you think for one moment I'm going to allow my ungrateful son to marry someone like you, then you are in for a rude awaking. So is he."

"Well goody for me. I don't much care for you either." Cassie turned to him then. "I guess she's going to be hanging around here. Can you have Noah just drop her things off at the hotel?"

"Yes, I can do that." Danburn was having a hard time keeping the mirth behind his teeth. He wished his mom was here...she'd be egging Cassie on and putting her two cents in with her, he knew it. "Come along then, family. We'll head home."

"I have never been treated this way in all my life. Since my son is remiss in doing as I told him, then I suppose I will have to go with you. But I'm not going to a hotel. I'm staying with him. He'll have to make room for me." Danburn told her that Cassie and Rett were living with him for the moment. "Together? What sort of brothel are you running, young man? He will not be staying with you. He'll have to rent a home now and a place for me to stay until I get him back to his old job and working again. There will be no more talk about marriage, nor him living with people I don't approve of."

"I guess it really sucks to be you if you think anyone is going to do what you wish. But if you want, I can pay for a return ticket home. Please let me do that for you. It would make my day to have you out of my hair." The two of them, Cassie and Elba, were going to be fun to watch. Dangerous as well, but a lot of fun. "If not, then shut the fuck up and enjoy the ride. I'm not one to mess with, lady. As you should have already figured out."

As they made their way out to the car, he could tell Elba was impressed by the limo. He knew her to be a greedy, vain woman, so it gave him a great deal of pleasure to ask about her limp. Danburn watched her entire body stiffen at the question.

"You're a very rude man, as I have pointed out before. There is nothing at all wrong with me. I took a short tumble, but I was able to get up and going just fine after." Danburn looked at it as they got in the car. "Where are you taking me? I'll have you know people are aware that I'm here. They'll come looking for me should you decide to try and harm me."

"What a vicious mind you have. I'm taking you to a hotel, as I said I was earlier. And you should have your ankle looked at. That tumble you took could be because your heels are too tall for a woman of your age." He knew he'd gone too far the moment the words left his mouth. Not that he cared, but he did hurt her. And as much as he disliked the woman, he didn't like to do that to anyone.

Danburn had expected her to retaliate, but not in the way she did. The cane that she'd been using hit him right across the cheek, and he felt it split open. He grabbed it from her before she hit him the second time, holding it above her head and she drew her hand back to slap him, but he caught her hand in his other one.

"You're very lucky that you're Rett's mother, because right now, I'd like nothing more than to beat you to death with this cane." Elba tried to take it from him again, and Danburn snapped it over his knee and tossed it to the floor. "Touch it and I will take great pleasure in killing you."

No one said a word. He felt his dragon move along his skin before he spoke to him. His voice was in deep contrast to the anger he could feel from the mighty beast.

She is not right in the head. I can feel such anger in her, more than is warranted for what has been done to her today. Also, you will need to help a young woman on the plane that she just left. I believe she wounded her as well. Danburn asked what happened. *The woman was speaking to the others around them and it upset this one. She hit her hard enough that she lost consciousness and is now being rushed to the hospital. I don't believe she is aware of what occurred.*

I'll take care of it. Can you keep me apprised of anything else she gets into while here? I need to make sure my family is safe, and that would include Cassie and Rett. He said that he would. *Do you know what her plans are while she is here?*

Yes. She is going to knock some sense into her ungrateful son.

That would not be Rett, would it? Danburn told him it was. *Ah, she is also going to try and forbid him to speak to his father. There is something there as well, just out of my reach for the moment. If you were to touch her in some way, I would be able to get more.*

I'll give it my best shot. But if my hands end up on her person, I'm not sure that I won't be tempted to strangle her. Dragon laughed and moved along his skin again. *I'm worried for him... Rett, I mean.*

He has a good mate, my lord. She will protect him in ways that even he will not realize. Also, you should be aware that Cassie's dragon is not what she seems. She is a dragon of the elements. A very rare and extremely old race.

Are you sure? He said that he was as positive as he'd ever been about anything. *Her kind, I thought they were all gone. I'm assuming that she's told Rett, hasn't she?*

Yes. And while he was a little disconcerted about the showing of what she could do, he has been very accepting of her as well. When she breeds, my lord, you will need to make sure that the babe is safe. There will be others out there that will wish to take it. He knew that as well. An elemental dragon could control all manner of earthly things. Danburn wondered if the earth knew. *She does, and is quietly making arrangements to keep her safe as well.*

When he asked his dragon to keep him informed, they were pulling up in front of the hotel. Danburn got out first, helped his wife and Cassie, and waited for Elba. He had a feeling that she was finding things not to her liking, and leaned his head in the door to ask if she was coming.

"I am not. I told you, I want to see my son. I don't plan to be here long enough to get settled in some snooty hotel that more than likely has more fleas than a cur dog." Danburn laughed.

"I should imagine that your mother is a woman of the streets, the way you act. Tell me, is she still living? If so, then I'd like to have a word or two with her about your behavior."

"She is, and I'd not fuck with her if I were you. My mother can be a real beast when necessary." Elba glared. "And if you ever call her a street walker again, I will turn you over to her. She isn't as nice as I am."

"Figures. But I'm not staying here. If you can afford this monstrosity of a car, then you can surely find me a nicer place to stay." He told her to get out or he'd do it for her. "You just wait, young man; I'm going to make you pay."

"Like you did George?" The look on her face told it all. "You should know that I'm having someone other than a person on your shit list look into things about that accident. It doesn't strike me as being on the up and up."

"You stay out of my family business, you hear me? Soon enough I'll have things the way they need to be. Whatever has happened is none of your concern. I won't warn you again." Danburn told her to get out of his car. "I'm going to ruin you, Danburn English. See if I don't."

"You can try, my dear, but I'm not nearly as young as I look, nor do I care one fig about how much money you have or think to have. I could buy and sell your puny ass ten times over and not have it bother me a bit." He put out his hand. "Now, would you like to do this the easy way, where you come out on your own? Or mine, where I reach in and snatch you out by your hair?"

She got out, but not with his help. Danburn was bothered by the meanness that she brought out in him, but also knew there were some people, like this woman, who needed to be shown who was boss. Normally he would have respected her for her age, been cordial to a fault, and offered her the opportunity to stay in his home simply because he had the room. But she made it difficult for him to even show the slightest bit of the niceties that he usually would have for her being Rett's mother.

Well, not always, but since Kendrick had come into his life. The love of his life had given him so much more to look forward to each day. Her smile, her laughter. Even the way she made all those wonderful noises when he made love to her. Having her in his life had given him one. A life worth living.

No wonder, Danburn thought, that Rett had such a low self-esteem, as well as a poor outlook for his own future. With a woman like his mother in his life, it was small wonder that he even managed to get away. Danburn would have run as far and fast as he could have if he had her in his life. When he got home, he decided to hug his mother tightly. Pulling out his phone, he decided it was well past time he had flowers delivered to her. And his lovely wife as well.

CHAPTER 5

Rett had no idea why he had agreed to do this. Mayor? He was barely making it as an attorney. What the hell was he supposed to do as mayor? When his name was called to go into the office, the man, Whitmore Clements, came out.

"I thought we could do lunch. I have to eat early or I won't be hungry for my wife's pot roast when I get home. You okay with that?" Rett was thrown for a moment, but said that was fine by him. "Good. There is this amazing diner in town. Have you eaten there yet?"

"No. Not yet. I've been trying to find a home to get settled into that my future wife and I can live in." Whitmore told him there would be a house with the job. "I'm sure that it's really lovely. About this job, Mr. Clements. I'm not sure that—"

"Call me Whit. Everyone does. Not my wife. For some reason she enjoys calling me by my given name. What's your future wife's name?" Rett told him. "I bet she's lovely too. Anyway, the house comes with the job, but if you find yourself something different, the city will pay up to a certain amount monthly for upkeep and such. The city also does all your repairs and lawn service. We can't have the mayor out mowing when the phone rings. There is also a good benefit package involved. I have to say, it's much better than normal towns have. Lord English kicks in a great deal by helping with that. We'll expect you to be available for all sorts of things as well. There are—"

"Wait. Just a second. You're acting as if I already have this job. I thought this was an interview." Whit told him the job is his. "I don't understand. Danburn said you were going to interview me. I thought.... Well, I thought you'd tell me thanks, but no thanks. You're not hiring me for this because of Danburn...Lord English, are you?"

"In a way, I guess. Not that he'd tell us to hire you. He'd never do that. But you did come with a great deal of experience in law. You're an intelligent man. Graduating at the top of your class from an Ivy League college is fantastic. But yes, to answer your question, he did play a part in us hiring you. When he recommends someone for a position, the entire town knows that it isn't going to get any better than that." Rett didn't know what to say. "You're going to do us well, Rett. We all know that. And you have no idea how glad we are that you're going to be the next mayor. When ours died quite suddenly last week, we had no idea what was going to happen to our place around here."

"I don't know what to say." Whit just smiled. "I'm new to this kind of work. I'll do the best that I can, but I'd like to have someone working with me. I don't know the town that well either."

"All taken care of. There is a committee that has volunteered to help you with that. I believe that Lady English—both of them, as a matter of fact—are a part of that group." They entered the diner and he felt his face heat up. A party was going on, apparently for him. "They wanted to start you off on the right foot, let you get to know some of the people here that you'll be dealing with on a long-term basis. I think they all have name tags on, but you go ahead and introduce yourself to them. And congratulations on the job, Mayor Rett. We're happy to have you here."

Rett met them all. He had actually gotten to know some of them over the last several days when he and Cassie were house hunting. Now a few things were becoming clearer to him as he talked to first the realtor that he'd used, then the grocer. They had known about this before him. He pulled out his cell phone after stepping outside for a breath of air. Cassie answered on the first ring.

"I have the job." She congratulated him, but he knew something was wrong. "What did my mother do to you?"

"Nothing that we can't handle, but she hit Danburn. Right across the face with her cane. He was a lot calmer about it than I would have been. And wow, can she be caustic when she wants to. How on earth did you live with her?" Rett told her he was sorry. "Oh, don't be. I'm actually having a blast now. She is not a nice person. I just don't understand how on earth you came from her."

"I often wonder the same thing." She asked him about the job. "It's a done deal. We have a house, servants, as well as someone to come and mow our lawn. And a cook. I'm not sure what your culinary preferences are, but I can't cook at all. Unless it has microwave instructions on it, I'm afraid we're going to starve."

Her laughter made him smile. "At one time in my many

lives, I was a chef. I loved it for a time, but like a lot of things that come with my age, I grew bored with it after a while. I think I've been just about everything there is to be. Even an attorney." He told her he thought she'd be good at that. "Not really. Every time I didn't win a case, I had to calm my inner beast not to go after someone. That might have gotten me into hot water a few times. I'm so proud of you, Rett. You're going to be the best mayor they've ever had. I know it."

He loved her. It hit him hard someplace between his head and heart. And Rett couldn't have been happier about it. Rubbing his hand over the place in his chest that only beat for her, he smiled.

"I'm in love with you. I mean, so much in love with you that I think I could easily die a very happy man right now." He heard her intake of breath. "I'm sorry. I don't know why I just blurted that out."

Before he could apologize again, she spoke. "I love you as well. I was just thinking of that when I realized what a horrid person your mother is and how you had grown up to be this wonderful, amazing man. I think even my dragon is in love with you. She certainly is a great deal quieter when you're around." She laughed again. "Which at the moment is a wonderful thing. Your mom is pissed off because the hotel we set her up in isn't what she wanted. I think she is under the impression that since Danburn has money, he should be putting her someplace better. I'm telling you right now, there won't be any kind of family Christmas cards where she must stand next to me given out. I might have to hurt her."

"No, we won't be doing that, I promise you. I'll have to thank Danburn for handling this for me. I could have rescheduled this interview, I suppose. But I might not have gotten the job if I'd had to deal with Mom and then come here for it. She would have ruined it for me, I think." He looked at the man who came out of the diner behind him. "Noah is here. I'm going to let you go now. I love you, Cassie."

"I love you too."

Rett looked at the man and could see that while he was concerned about something, he was also smiling.

"Something wrong?" Noah said that it was all good. "I'm not sure I believe that. I mean, you know that I've had a pretty good day so far. So if you could, whatever is wrong, can you give me a few more hours?"

"Nothing is wrong, My Lord. I did want to tell you that the house, your new home, is being cleaned by your new staff. I hope you don't mind, but I thought it would be helpful to you that it got started." He nodded. "A cook has been hired as well, by me. Not that I don't trust the town to do a good job, but I thought it important that you have someone that would be trustworthy. In the event someone had to shift and take to the skies."

Cassie. She would have to have someone in the household that wouldn't take her picture and sell it off to the highest bidder. He thought Danburn must have the same issues. Trust in something like this would be hard to come by.

"All right, I can understand that. I'm assuming you are taking care that the staff, whoever they are, will understand too. That we'll be safe in our house. Thank you for that." Noah grinned and nodded. "There's more, right?"

"Yes. The lady Cassie asked me to have some of her funds transferred to the bank here in this town. Also, to put your name to a few deeds as well. Credit cards and the like. I have them here when you're ready." Rett leaned back against the wall. He wasn't sure he wanted to ask. "You will need to know sooner or later, My Lord."

"I'm sure. But for now, why are you calling me that? I mean, I understand the lady part with Cassie. She's a dragon." Noah told him she was actually a lady; her family was royalty. "Of course they are. But I'm not. Let's deal with that later, shall we? Do I really need to know more today?"

"Yes. Her father, the duke of Windburg, is in town. I would suggest that you take Lord Danburn with you should you find yourself near him. He is, much to his dismay, lord over Windburg. I would imagine that Windburg feels no differently about my lordship. But as far as I know he knows nothing about you, and for the time being, I think that it would be best to keep it that way. I believe you will be safer because of that." Rett asked what exactly Danburn's title was. "He was Fletcher Danburn English, the ninth earl of the English Castle, until a long-lost uncle decided to.... Well, he is no longer with us. In doing so, Danburn is now the grand duke. He has inherited not just the title from this uncle, but a considerable fortune as well. *I'm* very happy to serve him as such."

"I take it he's not really thrilled about that?" Noah shook his head. "Noah, I don't know what I'm doing. I can quote law to someone. I know a little about a lot of things, but not enough to run a town. I have a mate that can change into a dragon, a good friend as well. You in my corner, which you have no idea how much I love knowing that. I think I feel out of my element right now."

"If you'd like my opinion, sir, I think that not only are

you suited for the position, but that you are going to do great things for this town. Also, there are a great many people who can help you. Men and women who believe not only that you're the right man for this position, but can do a good job at it. Your mate, I believe, loves you. And you her. What person could fail when he has so many willing to help without any qualms?" He told him he'd just discovered that he loved Cassie and she him. "Then you have everything you need to succeed."

"You're a good man, Noah. Does Danburn tell you that enough?" He told him sometimes he forgot. "Well, I hope you remind him of it. And often."

"I do, My Lord. I do." He grinned again. "If you are ready to face the new adventure in your life, I should like to take you to see a couple of houses, if you don't mind. Lady Cassie said to tell you that she has a great deal of things in storage if it comes to needing furniture. I'm to understand that it is some of the pieces of her life she has collected over time. Also, the cook, you should be aware is not human. He and his missus are both tigers. They will assist you in many things should you need it."

As they made their way through the throng of people, Noah told him all that he'd done. There was a great deal too. Credit cards, several of them, were handed to him, all new and shiny with his name on them. And he was given the specs on the home that the city had in mind, and the reason they were going to another home that would more suited to their needs. There was a car that came with his job with Danburn. A thick book of the bylaws of the town, as well as the name of his new secretary and driver when he needed him. There was also a list of people on several boards that he would be required to sit on, and the name of the tailor that would come to him in a couple of days.

"I'd like to see the house with Cassie. I know that it's likely more than we need, but if she has time, I'd like to see it with her for the first time." Noah told him she was on her way there now. "Good. Is there anything else pressing that I need to know?"

"Nothing pressing, no. But again, I want to warn you about Lady Cassie's father. He is not a man that you want to be around even on his better days. Which I am to understand there are few of those. It will not go well, I think. His name is Arlington, by the way, and he won't expect you to know Danburn...he will think you beneath him. He will also be surprised that you love his daughter. He isn't much different than your own mother in that he hates his child. He has found no use for her over the centuries until recently. I'm considering why now for you." Rett asked after her mom. "She has died, I'm afraid. No one is sure how, not even the earth Danburn has asked what caused her death, but we're looking into things. Sometimes, and it happens more often than not, a dragon will have met his or her death in the most peculiar way. She was a wonderful being, both as a woman and dragon. I knew her long ago, as I think Lady Elissa did. She was very magical as well, not counting the dragon. You would have liked her, and her you. As I said, a very wonderful woman. As is her daughter."

"Danburn told me that she had to have him step in to get her money back. Is that some of it?" He said that it was. "What will be required of me as man of the house, so to speak?"

80

"If you don't mind me saying so, sir, I think you will do well just simply to be yourself. You're a good man. Kind to others, and that shows in all that you do and say. If you would only do that, I think doors will open for you that otherwise might not have." Rett thanked him. "It is my pleasure to serve you, Lord Rett. You and Danburn are good men, and I think well of you both."

The ride to the newer house was informative. He knew now that he was worth more money, thanks to Cassie, than he'd ever have imagined. The house was one that the city had put up for sale some time ago, and Danburn had purchased it for very little money. But now it was his, a wedding gift for him and Cassie. The mayoral home wasn't suited for anyone that would have children, he'd been told.

~~~

Cassie stood on the front decking of the home and waited for Rett to join her. The yard was expansive, the trees that lined it and went around the home were huge and very old. She would gladly have spent her life out here if given the chance. But she was excited to see the inside of the big home, especially with Rett at her side.

The kiss that he gave her as soon as he reached the deck was wonderful. And had they not had others around, she might have shown him just how much she enjoyed him too. Noah asked to be excused in showing the house, as he had to go on an errand for his lordship, and left them alone. Cassie wrapped her arms around Rett as Noah returned to the car and sped away.

With the instructions to call if there were any problems, Cassie and Rett stood at the doorway to what might be their new home. Cassie wanted to beg Rett to hold her, tell her things were going to be all right, but he only had to take her hand into his and she felt everything balance out.

She was in love with her mate, and things in the rest of the world could just fuck off as far as she was concerned. Cassie decided that she didn't want to ruin this by being unsure or afraid, but she was both those things and more. This was their first home, and she wanted it to be perfect.

As soon as they entered the three story house, Cassie was in love with it. And it appeared that Rett was as well when he whistled loudly upon entering. There was a grand entrance, one that screamed to her that the house had been built with grandeur and money. She moved to the right with Rett, and the room it spilled into was as glorious as any library she'd ever been in. Tall shelves from ceiling to floor surrounded the room. A fireplace was banked on both sides with doors and windows that were as large as the shelving. In the middle of the room was a large desk, facing not just the fireplace but the yard beyond the doors. She could almost see Rett sitting behind it, talking on the phone or using the computer as he did his job.

There was no other furniture in the room, and she made her way to the desk when she saw the envelope on the top. Picking it up, she read it to Rett as he moved to the shelves that were as old as the house.

"The desk comes with the house. Apparently, the previous owners couldn't decide on how to get it out of here without knocking down a wall and left it for us. Do you like it?" He said that he did, very much so. "Then I guess it'll make a great desk for the new mayor."

"Look at these books they left too. First additions. Why would someone do that?" She pulled one of them off the shelf and opened it. "Do you like to read?"

"Oh yes. Very much so. And some of these authors, I've actually met. I have numerous crates of my own books that will look good in here too."

They made their way to the next room, the living area, and found another fireplace, as well as windows and doors, like in the library, which she knew would offer a spectacular view year round. She could see a pool, and walked to one of the doors that led out to it. Again, there wasn't any furniture, not that she cared. There was plenty of time for them to fill it with things they liked if he decided the things she had weren't what he wanted. More than anything, Cassie wanted Rett to be happy.

"I have some things in storage. I asked Noah to tell you that." Rett said that he did and was happy that she had it. "We can go through it if you want, see what we can use here. I think there are some living room things, as well as several bedroom sets. I guess this place has nine."

"Yes. Noah told me that even though the house is very old, the owners made a great many improvements to it. There are also six bathrooms, not counting the two down here, as well as the master suite." She asked him if he was ready to see the next room. "I wanted to tell you something first. About this house and what I can give it. I have nothing."

"You have everything." He shook his head. "Do you mean that you think you have nothing to put here? Well you do. You have whatever I have. Everything is ours now, and it matters little me to if you never work again. You won't have to if you don't want to, but I like being out in the world."

"As do I. This mayor job, it's not anything I might have applied for had it not been for Danburn, but I think I might enjoy it. For a time." She nodded and told him they had plenty of that now. "Yes. I guess we do."

Hand in hand they explored the rest of the house. There was a large dining room with built in china cabinets. The kitchen was up to date and modernized, also big enough to plan and cook for a large number of guests. She loved the herb garden that was just outside the door, and a spacious walk in freezer that was there as well.

The bedrooms were all empty for now on the upper floors. The bathrooms were gorgeous, and roomy enough to not just have a tub in each one, but a walk-in shower as well. As they made their way to the master suite, which was on the uppermost floor, she reflected on how much work it was going to be to keep the place clean. She told Rett she wasn't sure she was up for the task.

"I guess we have staff." Before she could tell him that might not work, he continued. "Noah hired them. He told me he was going to make sure they're well versed in taking care of a home with a dragon in it. Also, our cook is a cat, as is his mate. We're pretty much taken care of other than bringing your things here."

The master suite was beautiful. And it was furnished. Again, there was a note, telling them that it had been much too large for them to move and they had decided to leave it behind. Rett sat on the bed and smiled at her.

"We could christen the house now if you want. I don't know about you, but I think we should test this bed out before we decide on the home. That way, if it's not up to par, we can move on to something else. What do you think?" She laughed and walked slowly to him. "I think we could easily christen the entire house today the way I feel about you. I love you so much."

"Will you make love to me?" He stood up. "Not sex. We have sex a lot, but I want you to take your time, hold me, make love to me."

He kissed her then. Taking his time, just the way she wanted. And when he lifted his head and looked at her, she fell so much more in love with him that it took her breath away. When he stepped back, she stood still before him.

Rett unbuttoned her blouse, slowly, kissing the exposed area as he revealed it. Once he had her completely on display, the blouse opened to the hem, he pulled it off and dropped it to the floor. As he ran his finger up her ribs and just under her breasts, he kissed her shoulders, neck, and ears.

Cassie couldn't breathe. Her lungs, along with her heart, stopped working properly. Then when she thought she wasn't going to be able to stand up on her own two feet, he kissed her again, this time making her whimper when he pulled back.

"When I was about seventeen, I met this…well, this woman who was a good deal older than me. She took me to her bed. I was eager, don't get me wrong, but she taught me that words used while making love to someone are just as important as the physical aspect of it." He unhooked the front closure on her bra, barely touching her skin as he did so. "To me it seemed silly. But now, with you, all I can think about is telling you just how much I love everything about you."

"Oh Rett, I love you so much." The bra was off and on the

floor by her blouse. When he dropped to his knees in front of her, she held her breath. "What are you going to do to me?"

He looked up at her. His face, his beautiful face, was in total concentration. But it was the words that he spoke, the way he said them to her, that made her feel his love. The simple word, "Everything," had her body humming for his touch.

Her pants came off as slowly as her blouse had, his fingers seeming to burn into her flesh with each brush of them. Cassie could feel her heart pounding, her skin tightening in anticipation of what he might do next. Whatever it was, she was going to enjoy it. Then when he kissed each of her hips, describing how they tasted, she felt her pussy soak, her nipples ache. This was the way a man made love to a woman, with everything that he was.

"Your skin tastes like I think roses would with the first bloom of the season. It feels like warm sun soaked tomatoes on the vine. Firm and ripe." He pulled her panties off. "Your smell makes me think of fresh air after a nice storm. Snow on mountains. Your warmth is like a blanket I can snuggle under on a cold winter night."

"Rett, please." He didn't laugh at her desperation. "I need you."

"Yes, I can smell you. Feel you." He kissed her thigh, her knee, and rubbed his hand over her calf and shin. Then he slid his hand up her thigh again and into her pussy. "Come for me, Cassie."

She screamed. The climax was so powerful and so long that she was weak with it. But she needed more, the everything he'd promised her and then some. Even as she felt her body building up again, he took her pussy in his mouth and suckled her clit. Cassie came apart four more times before he stood.

When he picked her up in his arms, she held him. As he laid her out on the bed, she watched him strip to his bare skin before he joined her there. He kissed her again as his body rolled over her.

"You are the greatest thing that has ever happened to me. Ever." He held her hands in his larger ones, his fingers laced with hers. "I love you, Cassie. With all that I am."

He filled her. Not just entered her, but filled her from head to toes. As she watched his face, his body took hers, over and over, giving her more than just himself, but everything about him. And when he kissed her again, this time feeding her body with something extra, she cried out as she came. It was then that Cassie let the darkness take her under.

CHAPTER 6

The clinic was busy. Danburn was looking over some of the invoices, just to make sure there was still enough money in the business account to pay them all. He looked at his mom when he heard arguing outside the door. She told him to wait just where he was and listen.

Cocking his head so he could figure out who was with the male voice, he realized that his door was no longer closed like it had been. His mom, he'd bet, had opened it up enough so as he could hear whatever was going on.

"You'll do things my way or I'll just ban you from staying here." Danburn stared at his mom as the man's voice carried into his office. "There are rules here, and I make them as I see fit. If you don't care for the way things are run, then leave. It'll just be more for the rest of us when you do."

"I was told that I could come here for a shower and some food. Are you telling me that I can't have that now?" The other voice laughed. "I don't think this is the way that Miss Kendrick meant for things to work out for us here. And I'm betting that Miss Cassie willll be fit to be tied when she finds out what you're doing."

"Well, do you see her around? Do you think that she cares one fucking bit whether or not you were able to get food? I'll tell you, no she doesn't. And neither do I. You give me what you have on you now, and I might see my way into letting you wash some of the stink off you." He heard the second man talking as they moved away, their voices fading into nothing.

"How long has this been going on? And how long have you known?" His mom got up and handed him a thumb drive and asked him to put it in his computer. "I'm assuming that Kendrick doesn't know about this."

"No. She hasn't been made aware of it yet. I didn't know either until Cassie approached me. She's been telling me that the doctor here has been having some issues, but she'd never say what. Then the day before yesterday, she handed me this and her resignation. I don't believe she thinks anyone will take care of this." He put the drive in his computer and it showed a man towering over one of the residents, hitting him. "That man's name is Timothy, as you might well know. And his friend the doctor — Walter, I believe his name is — isn't any better. The two of them have been running this place as their own little hit squad since they arrived. And before you ask, I don't know why Cassie didn't say anything before now. I do believe, however, that she has a good reason."

"A good reason for letting others be hurt?" She said that she had one in that she didn't trust any of them. "Why not? What did we ever do to her to make her think that?"

"You're her lord." He started to say he was her friend as well, but his mom continued. "When she arrived here, she had to pay homage to you. You didn't require it, I'm sure, but you took it. You more than likely didn't think anything of it.

90

It is what you would do to any other dragon that comes here. But since then, have you done much in the way of making her feel like she's more than just a subject of yours?"

"No. I don't...haven't. I could say that it never occurred to me, but that's not much better." Mom said that it wasn't. "So she let this happen, knowing it wasn't right."

"You and Kendrick let this happen when you hired those men without checking on their references well enough. And I do believe that she took care of it as best she could. Watch the rest of the drive." He glanced down in time to see Cassie confronting the man that had beaten one of the homeless.

There was no sound on the cameras that had been installed. It had been on his list of things to replace, but as he watched, he wished he had done it sooner. She was obviously screaming at the man, and when he hit her, his fist connecting with her face, he wanted to go there now and take care of the man. Instead, he let his beast calm before looking at his mom.

"He hurt her." She nodded. "I have to do something. And I have no idea why, but I think you know just what has to be done."

"Oh yes, I do. I have a plan if you'd be nice enough to let me take care of this, I'll make sure that this never happens again." Danburn nodded and smiled. "You have to help, of course, there is no getting around that, but I want to take care of this with young Cassie."

"You said she quit." Nodding, his mom told him she had one more day to work. "All right. Then when do we take care of these pieces of shit?"

"In about an hour."

He was told to stay in the offices, that no one knew he

91

was there. As he went over the rest of the paperwork in front of him, he watched the monitors that were connected to the computer in his office. Something he should have been doing a lot more, he realized now, was keeping a better eye on things and helping when he could. But he'd been busy. No, that wasn't the right word, distracted. He should have at least taken care that Cassie knew he would be there when she needed him. Danburn knew that he was long past due in talking to her about a great many things.

He told Kendrick what was going on and how his mother had a plan, but he wasn't privy to it yet. Kendrick pointed out that Cassie was afraid of them both. That she thought in Cassie's mind that they were her bosses, and she was nothing more than a servant to them.

How do you figure that? We've had them both over. I've welcomed her to the family. I think you might have read it wrong. She didn't say anything. *Okay, Miss Smarty Pants. Why do you think that?*

Have you noticed that she only sits when we're both sitting? And when she does, it's on the floor or she slouches down so that she's lower than your eyes? Or that she never looks you in the eye? He said that he'd not. *Also, she never speaks her mind as she does with others when you're around. Me either, for that matter. She's subservient to us. And as much as I hate to admit it, I was kind of liking it. But no more. We're hurting her and Rett by not thinking of them as our equals. As friends.*

He hated that too. And since she'd pointed it out to him, he thought of other times she'd been like that to him. When he'd gone to talk to her about her father, she sat on the floor. Another time when his mom had been in the room, Cassie had stood so stiff he thought she was in pain.

Danburn was embarrassed he'd not noticed what was right there in front of him all along. But he wasn't sure how to make her stop. It was well past time, he knew, and he was going to make sure that everyone did, as well, that she and Rett were family, as close as blood.

Mom left him not long after he spoke with Kendrick, saying she'd be back, but for him to remain in his office until she was there. He told her he would but he didn't like it. Kendrick wanted to be there too, but Mom told her to stay back. If they messed this up, they might not get another chance to fix it.

"Well, I don't like this, just so you know. But for now, I'll do as you ask." His mom kissed him and started for the door, only to pause.

"Danburn, when the time comes, you're to step back out of your role as king dragon and just be a backup. I promise you, great things will come from it if you do." He nodded and said that he would. "I love you, son. I truly do."

So, there he sat, getting nothing done but feeling badly because of his lack of keeping on top of things. But that was going to change, right away. He started on a list of things to make this place safer too.

He was going to have to have Noah find someone that would make the monitors show up at his home. Also, he needed to speak to Pierce, his own physician, to see if he knew of anyone that could come here and work. There was no doubt in his mind that they'd be short a man or two before this was over.

His phone started ringing just as Kendrick came in his office by way of the window. He picked it up after asking her to have a seat. It was his mom. She told him to wait for her to come and get them both. After hanging up, he told Kendrick what he knew.

"She told me to come here, but to wait until the coast was clear before heading to your office. It was her idea to come in that way. Kind of fun if you ask me. I thought that she was joking at first, but I have to tell you, she is one scary dragon when she has her mind set on something." Danburn said he was well aware of that. "I figured you would be. Do you know anything else?"

"Not yet. Other than we're to wait here for her." He wasn't sure about any of this and told her that.

"I'm sure that whatever your mom has in mind, it's going to be safe. And if not, you can call out your big, bad dragon and get rid of the evidence." He wasn't sure if she was serious or not. Sometimes he still didn't get sarcasm, even though she told him daily that he was the king of it.

"I don't think I like the way your mind is working this out. You've become very mercenary lately." He laughed when she did. "Do you suppose we should have a talk with Cassie and Rett? I've been thinking more and more about what Mom told me."

"I think if we did, they'd shit themselves with worry. No. We'll figure out a way to make this work, but calling them to the house or wherever might make it worse." He nodded. "Besides, it sounds like your mom has it all worked out anyway."

He hoped so. Looking at his monitor, he saw Cassie coming down a long hall, followed by both Timothy and Walter. His mom called and told him to meet her and the rest of them in the main hall were Cassie was.

The argument was in full swing when he arrived. Standing back with Kendrick beside him, he waited for the right moment to make sure they saw him. But that fell through the moment Timothy decided he was going to win at all costs. Just as Timothy drew back to no doubt hit Cassie, Danburn grabbed his hand and twisted it up behind him.

"Danburn? I had no idea you were here today. I'm glad you are, however. You should know that we caught her stealing." He looked over at Cassie when Walter spoke, like they had this planned or something. "Tim was just telling her to give it back when she spit on us."

"Spit? Where? I don't even see a spot on either of you." Danburn looked at Kendrick. "Did you see anyone spitting?"

"No. I don't think I did." She nodded to Cassie and spoke to him through their link. *She's not going to be able to help us out with her face planted in the floor like that.*

She was too. Her body was flat on the floor and her hands spread out, as if she were awaiting some sort of punishment. When he said her name gently, she told him she hadn't stolen anything.

"I'd very much like for you to stand and speak to me, please." He'd not used any kind of compulsion with her. He didn't want to have to either. After a time she finally stood up, but wouldn't look at him, and that disturbed him more than he could say. "Cassie, have these men been giving you any trouble?"

Before she could answer, if she was going to, Walter spoke, his voice high and tight. The man looked like he might have tried to hit her again, but caught himself just in time. "Us giving her trouble? Did you know she's been stealing drugs? And that—" Danburn shook the man in front of him hard enough to rattle his teeth. Walter looked at Timothy, then up at Danburn, calmer now. "You can't possibly believe anything she tells you, Danburn. She's not fit to be here."

"Not fit? How the hell do you think that?" He started to kick them both out when he glanced at Cassie, then back at his mate. This was what his mother had been talking about. A way for Cassie to know that he had her back. "Cassie is my... well, not my blood, but closer, she's my sister-in-law. She and Rett are my family."

Cassie looked at him then. She had the most surprised look on her face, and Danburn knew that this was what his mom had planned. When she started to drop her head again, Danburn said her name.

"Cassie, honey, tell me, why was he going to hit you? I mean, he'd better have more of an excuse than that you were stealing from this place. I know better." She looked at the two men, then back at him. "I will believe you over them any day of the week. I promise you this. But without your help, I can't fix whatever is going on here."

~~~

Cassie felt her dragon run over her body. She was protecting her, she knew that, but she was having a difficult time calming her and trying not to submit to Danburn. She opened her mouth to tell him it was all right, but something snapped inside of her and she told him the truth instead. Letting out a long held breath, she told Danburn what she had been seeing over the last few weeks.

"They're hurting the people that come here for help.

Everyday it's something else with them. But mostly it's when Timothy gathers up the homeless and Walter feeds from them. Then they take their money or whatever they might have that he finds worthy. After that, he beats them until they can't move or kills them. Last week he started charging for them to take a shower, and makes them all use the same towel." She felt her dragon again, this time embracing her in comfort. "But that's not all. I mean, there is something else you should know."

"What?" Danburn looked at her, and she had a feeling that while he was pissed off, it wasn't directed at her. "You know something and I'd very much like for you to share it with me. Will you please tell me?"

She asked him to follow her. The two men, the vampire and the wolf, were to be detained by security. Cassie knew they were on the payroll of these two men and told Danburn that. So they all, including security, came along with them to the storage room.

"She's the one you should be having in your grip. I'm sure that whatever she tells you about that room has not a shred of truth to it." Timothy started to back away but Kendrick held him. "I have done nothing wrong here. I quit."

"You move from that spot, and so help me you'll wish that you were being brought before your alpha instead of me." Kendrick looked at her again as she continued. "Go ahead, Cassie. Show us what you know."

Opening the door to the storage room, she stood back while the others entered. There wasn't much to see in the big room where they were. Most of what was going on had to do with the back of it, but things missing here as well. Petty stuff compared to what she knew was going on.

As she pointed out the lack of supplies, toilet paper that had been taken, as well as other things that were donated or bought, she explained to them what she knew was happening. Blankets had been sold over the Internet. Cassie also told them about the other things that had come up missing, such as the shelf which was to hold extra clothing and medical supplies.

"Where is it?" Danburn was pissed. It was showing on every part of his body. He shook Walter again, and the man continued to blame her for the missing things. "I swear by all that is holy, you're going to pay for this. Tell me where the items are that are supposed to be on these shelves."

"Ask her." Kendrick touched her fingers to Danburn's arm and he calmed. A little anyway. Walter laughed as if he'd won and continued. "She is the one that has been fucking with the inventory. I think you should maybe consider looking at her house. I've been looking over things here, Danburn. You must believe me. It's all her, I swear it."

"There's more." Danburn said for her to show him. But when he stretched his neck, the popping sound loud in the mostly empty room, she took a step back from him. "Don't hurt me, please. If you want to know, I've given my notice. I won't work in this sort of place where people are hurt and I can't do anything about it."

"I'm going to do something about it right now. I swear to you, as pissed off as I am, not one bit of it is directed at you." She watched his dragon move over his skin and she took another step back. When he let out a hot breath, she felt her own dragon move quickly over her. She'd come out, she knew it, if Danburn tried to harm her. Then she knew they'd

98

both be dead. "He can talk to me. Does yours talk to you?"

"No. Well, yes, but not like another person." He asked her what she meant. "I can feel her guiding me. Directing me to where she thinks I'll be safer. But we never converse like humans do."

"What is she telling you now?" Cassie told him she thought that he was going to hurt someone, and she hoped it wasn't her. "I swear it won't be you. Your dragon, she knows that I'm going to protect you. No matter what. These men? They're as good as dead as far as I'm concerned. And they more than likely will be once I call their masters. You show me what it is you've discovered, and I promise you, the only person that is going to be in trouble is these two."

Cassie wanted to believe him. Needed to, actually. And other than run, which would mean that she'd be running for the rest of her life, she turned to the back of the warehouse to show them what she'd found several days ago.

"They went to a lot of trouble to make sure that no one knew about it. I mean, I'm sure to their way of thinking, no one would miss a few old people, now would they?" She was babbling, but right now thought it was better than sucking her thumb in a corner. "I have a list of the ones that went missing. I did it before I knew what was going on. I thought that someone was taking them for other things, like their checks or something. But I never in all my dreams expected to find this and how they were being killed."

She pushed open the door and gagged. The smell always made her do that, the odor of blood and death. When both Danburn and Kendrick moved by her, she watched their faces. It was horrific, she knew, but it wasn't as bad as she'd seen before.

"This vampire, Walter, he's done this before. Through the centuries, I mean. I might not have remembered him at all but for the fact that I found this in here. I ran into him once before when a similar scene took place in a large town. It took me a little while to remember him...I think he's changed his appearance somehow. I was going to let you know about it tomorrow, when Rett and I were out of town for good. I didn't want him to be in trouble with you too."

Walter started speaking to her, in a language that she didn't know, but apparently Kendrick did.

"He said to tell you that he should have killed you long ago." Cassie nodded. There were times, she told him, that she wished he had. "Also, you should know that he's going to get you after this. I'm not sure how he figures that's going to happen now that Danburn has him, but who knows the mind of a fool."

She looked around the room as Danburn and Kendrick did, seeing things that she'd missed before. The containers of blood that would do no one any good, especially the vampire that needed it. The clothing that they had on, even some of the supplies that were missing were here too. To mop up the blood of their victims.

These men had taken the homeless and downtrodden and hung them here. Killed them for no other reason than that they could, their necks slashed and their blood flowing into a large vat. She had no idea why anyone would do such a thing. She'd read somewhere that once the blood was tainted with air, it was no longer any good to a vampire. Or perhaps that was the point.

Three men showed up just as Danburn came back to the front of the room. She knew them to be wolves, the larger of the three the alpha. She didn't even feel sorry for the man who was now in his clutches. In fact, she was glad that he'd come in person and not sent one of his men.

When the other two men took the begging and screaming Timothy away, the alpha turned to her. He bowed low and then took her hand in his. She knew what he was about to do, so took her hand back from him.

"I have a mate." He nodded once. "I don't need anything from you for this. I know that you feel you owe me, but as I said, I have a mate and he will have to approve whatever it is you do."

"I have spoken to Rett just moments ago. He and I go back a long way. My name is Shawn Canon. Rett is a good man; you could not do better in having him as your mate." She told him that she agreed. "He said that should I feel that I want to reward you...no, not reward, but thank you for your help in this, that I should ask you. And if I did anything untoward to you, I should expect you to burn me to a crisp. Rett is of the opinion that I might make you upset with me."

"I don't care all that much for people." He laughed, throwing back his head with his laughter. "Are you making fun of me?"

"Nay, I am not. I'm merely a man thinking that you will be a delightful addition to my pack. You and young Rett." She asked him how old he was, knowing that this was not a wolf one would tangle with. "Older than the trees that surround my home. I am one of the first wolves. The blood of my family runs through every wolf shifter ever born. We're the oldest

101

known to any pack."

"The Canon wolves." He bowed before her and then stood. "I've heard of your kind. It's said that you can shift not just into a wolf, but one that even other shifters cannot tell the difference between man and beast."

"That is very true." He took her hand in his again and she didn't take it back. "I should like to give you a gift. A thank you for your help."

"I didn't do this for that." He said that he knew that about her as well. "Will the man…will Timothy be killed?"

"It is done." She nodded. The law of pack was to not harm anyone that didn't harm you. She thought it was a good rule. But she knew the Canon pack for something more. Something that most had no idea of. They made the laws that governed all wolves, as her family had done for dragons. And like hers, punishment for breaking the rules was death. Which was swift. "May I?"

"Yes. But in return, I would like a favor of you." He said anything. "You might not think so when I ask. The elderly in this building, they are lonely for company. Of any kind. You have smaller pack members, children that could benefit from human contact. I'd like for you to allow them to come here, to be canine companions to them. To ease the days they might have left on this earth."

"Will they need to know that we are shifters? Some will, I think, but not all." She said that unless they wanted to tell them, then she wouldn't. "Then it is a deal, Casandra Welsh."

The lick of his tongue over the back of her hand was rough, his saliva numbing what he was going to do. The bite, one that would mark her as friend to his pack, wouldn't be painful, but it would be visible to anyone that had any kind of magical powers. As soon as he stepped back, he bowed once again.

"You need only to call out to me. You or your family. We are forever indebted to you. Also, Lord Markum will be to see you soon as well." She asked who that was. "The vampire that also owes you."

The humans were taken down, their bodies wrapped in soft blankets to be taken out for burial. Danburn said that he would make sure they were taken care of and markers of the ones that they could identify put with them. The security guards were taken care of by the leaders of their respective clans. Cassie was sure it was certain death to them all. It took them four gruesome hours to clean up the scene, and then Danburn turned to her.

"I should like your help in cleaning this area up. My dragon is very large and will.... Well, you could imagine what sort of damage he could do. If you'd be so kind as to burn this part of the building out, I'd be indebted to you." She told him that it would be her pleasure, but he owed her nothing. "Ah, but I do. You saved me a great deal of heartache with this. And had the authorities found out, they would have shut this place down. The fact that we can take care of it on our own means there are others that can and will get help from here. Pierce, my own doctor, is getting a replacement for Walter as well."

They both looked over at Walter. His hands were bound in silver, and he'd been tied to a post. If she had her way, he'd be here when she took care of his mess by burning him with all the rest of the trash, and be done with him. But she had a feeling that his master, Lord Markum, would enjoy taking care of the man himself.

When he was jerked up from the floor after being unleashed, he went along with Danburn and Kendrick out the door. The only one left with her was the Canon alpha, and his grin made her think he had something in mind.

"I know what you are." She nodded, figuring that he would. "I'm assuming that Danburn does not?"

"No. I mean, it's never come up." He nodded. "Are you going to blackmail me or something? I have to tell you, I won't pay it."

"I have no use for money. Nor do I plan to take anything else from you. So untrusting. What I would enjoy is to see you use your magic. For one as old as me, it will be a rare treat to see such a thing." He grinned larger. "You will learn to trust those here, Casandra. Of this I am certain."

Shifting to her dragon, she let her go. There was no pain in being separated into the others, but she would lead them. As they moved around the room, taking care not to burn through the walls that were there, Cassie made sure that no one, not even a vampire that came here, would ever smell or feel the death of the others. Only the few that were here, who had seen it, would ever know.

When she was finished, she made her way back to the big alpha, and without a word he bowed once again and left. She wondered if she should trust him or not, but she had a feeling she could. If not, then she'd take care of him later.

CHAPTER 7

Elba sat in the lobby waiting for someone to come and pick her up. She'd been told by some flunky in a uniform that there would be a car for her shortly. Shortly? It had been over ten minutes she'd been down here waiting. Apparently that word didn't have the same meaning to some people as it did her.

"Idiots. Every last one of them." She shifted on her seat. It was very comfortable to her sore bottom, but she didn't want anyone here to know that. She knew they'd take advantage if they thought they were getting one up on her.

Elba had tried calling her son several times since she arrived here two days ago. The phone number that she'd had was now disconnected, and there didn't seem to be any way for her to get the new one. She knew that he had to have a phone; he was forever on it when she saw him.

It had been a few months since she'd seen Everette. In a way she was glad for that, but she realized that without any way of communicating with him, she had no way to put him in his place. The ungrateful boy had to get his life together and start sucking up or she'd be even madder at him than she was now. While thinking of her son, she thought of her husband.

The parole board had contacted her again, not that she returned either their emails or phone calls. Elba had an idea what they were going to tell her, and she just didn't want to hear it. She didn't want her husband out, and they'd better not go above her head to get it done. He was fine just where he was. And she wasn't going to talk to them about it.

What was it, she wondered, that got them all fired up to let him out after all this time? The man had admitted to killing two people in a drunken rage, hadn't he? He'd run them right over. Elba shifted on the seat again and felt the pain of her ankle run up her leg to her belly.

She'd fallen again. Getting out of the bathtub just last night, she'd reached for the towel rack and missed it. Her entire life had flashed before her eyes as she fell backward, and when she'd hit her head on the tile behind her, it had blinked her out faster than she could have cried for help.

When she woke, cold and in pain, it had taken her an hour to not just get up off the cold floor, but out of the bathroom as well. She hurt…not just her head, which had bled most of the night, but her ankle ached very badly now. Even to put weight on it made her slightly sick to her belly. But Elba wasn't one to complain, and made her way around the cheap hotel as if nothing was wrong.

When a man sat beside her she turned to tell him to get out of her space. But there was something…. It took her several moments to realize who it was. It was her son, and something had happened to him. Something she was sure she wasn't going to like, and her hands itched to slap the smile right off his face.

"What have you done, Everette? You look like a fool." He laughed, and that ticked her off more. "You certainly have made me dance a jig here. You're going to do as I say now and book us a flight home today. Right now. That is, if you can get your head out of your bottom long enough. I do not care for the way you've been acting of late, Everette. And as of this very moment, you'll do as I tell you. Get to it."

"No. And I'm not going anywhere, Mother. You can if you wish, but I find that I like it a great deal right where I am." She told him she didn't care what he wished. "I know that. You never have. It's sad really, to think how much you've made those around you as bitter as you are. You almost had me too, but I found happiness, and you're not going to fuck that up."

"Why you.... You cannot speak to me that way. I demand that you apologize this minute." He only laughed and stood up. "Everette, I'm not at all happy with you at the moment. You've made me come here, and then you've ignored me for some tart that doesn't know her place. I will not have you marrying either, so you can get that notion right out of your head as well."

"I didn't make you come here, you did that on your own. As for the woman...yes, Cassie is what takes up most of my time. I'm in love. And believe it or not, I no longer want your opinion, nor do I ask for it. Not that it ever stopped you from giving it, but I have no reason to listen to you anymore." She huffed at him. "You don't believe in love, Mother?"

"I do not. It's a worthless emotion that should have been bred out of people a long time ago. What has it gotten anyone? Nothing. Even you were a disappointment to me. No, I've told you what to do and you'll do it. And there will be no more talking to your father. That man isn't right in his head."

"He's here." She paused in rising from the couch, ready to tell him to have her bags packed. "Dad is here, in town. I have some friends that pulled a few strings, and he's out for good. Not that he should have ever been in prison in the first place, but that's going to be fixed as well. There is evidence that he wasn't the one responsible for the death of those people. I don't suppose you'd like to tell me just what happened that night, would you?"

"What are you talking about? Of course, he was. He confessed, didn't he?" He only stared at her. "What has he told you? That it was me? He's a drunk and a liar. I was nowhere near that accident when it happened. Whoever told you that is a deceiver. I have witnesses that say I was at home when he did that horrific thing."

"Dad told a different story than the one you did. And when an attorney friend of mine went back to check your claims, ones where you said you were at home, the neighbors were relieved to find that you weren't there to bully them. One even said you held his child in your basement in order to get them to lie for you." Everette tsked at her. "You should take better care that there are no recordings of what you do from now on, Mother. It might have saved you a bit of jail time. Imagine our surprise when not only did he have proof that you blackmailed him, but that you made sure he stayed in line all these years with the threat of killing him and his family."

She sat down. It was that or fall. Every part of her body hurt, and she was pretty sure that Everette was aware of that as well. Elba looked up at him, seeing something she'd never seen on his face before. The look his father would givewhen he was angry with her.

Stiffening her back bone, making sure to look him in the eyes when she spoke, Elba thought of all the things she was going to have to take care of when she returned to her home. And she would too, just as soon as she dealt with this child of hers.

"I don't have any idea what those fools said. They're all fornicators and drunks. All of them are on welfare of some kind, and will do anything for a dollar or two. Why they'd say those things about me just goes to show what sort of people they are." She stood up again, leaning heavily on her cane. "I've had enough of this town and of you thinking you can boss me around, Everette. We're going back today and I'll straighten them all out."

She would too, starting with that brat of her neighbor's. He was going to suffer badly, and all because of his stupid parents. Elba wasn't a murderer—she didn't count it as murder when they died later—but she would make him hurt in ways that would have him thinking twice about crossing her. She was about half way to the elevator when she realized she was alone. Turning back to her son, she asked him what the delay was.

"Delay? None that I know of. But if you think I'm going with you, anywhere, then you're nuts." She slammed the cane down, wishing he was close enough for her to hit. "I see you replaced the other one. You shouldn't hit people who are bigger than you. And with more money. Danburn is the one that is helping us along with Dad's conviction. It's a lot easier to get things done when you have a person like him in your corner."

She had to get out of town before he said, or for that matter figured out, too much. And he would too, she knew it. The boy had no respect for her, and he'd lie, to everyone, just to get away from her. Well, she had news for him, she didn't want him in her life either. Going the rest of the way to the elevator alone, she thought of all the things she was going to need to do.

She would have to call the airport on her own. And pack. There was no way she was going to let any of these fools help her. Then there was the added expense of hiring a car to take her not just to the airport, but to her home when she got back there. Or she'd have one of the fools near her home come and get her or know her wrath.

Just as the doors slid open, she felt someone touch her shoulder. Turning, lifting the cane to knock some sense into the jack wipe, she felt it ripped from her hands before she could hit him.

"What do you think you're doing? Give me back my property right this minute." The officer, some suck up, she didn't doubt, just stepped back out of her reach. "Did you hear me? Are you stupid? I said to give me back my cane."

"Elba Wayne Welsh? I'm here to take you in for questioning." She said she wasn't going anywhere with him. "Oh, but you are. You can go easily or hard. It's entirely up to you."

"You touch me and I will own everything you have. Even that tiny penis of yours. Now, hand me my walking stick and get away from me." Before she could reach the man, she saw three others coming toward her. "What is the meaning of this?

I'm here to visit my son, then I'm going home."

"You have the right to remain silent...." As he droned on about her rights, all she could think about was how he was going to pay for this, for violating her rights by detaining her. Elba knew the law better than most did, and these fools were going to answer for this. Then she was going to make her son pay. He was the one causing all these unnecessary delays. "Do you understand these rights as they have been told to you, Ms. Welsh?"

"You will not be taking me anyplace, do you hear me? I'm on my way home." He said nothing but rocked on his heels and smiled. "If I had my cane, I'd wipe that smirk right off your face."

"Are you threatening me, Ms. Welsh?" She told him she most certainly was. "Did you know that's against the law? That threatening an officer of the law is a punishable offense?"

"You just come a little closer and I'll add abuse to it as well."

She found herself on the floor then, her entire body being pressed into the cold tile like she was to become some sort of bizarre art project. If she hadn't hurt before this, she knew she was going to when she got up. But the best part was, so would the little crapper that tossed her here.

As she was being led away, she looked for Everette. He was the one that was responsible for this, sticking his nose into things that didn't pertain to him. And when she found him, he was standing next to the mouthy woman from the day she'd gotten here.

"Everette, unhand that tart and come here and tell these men that I'm your mother. I swear to you, when I return home heads are going to roll. I'm going to hire myself a good attorney and sue the pants off these monsters." He told her he was an attorney. "Not you. I'm going to hire a good one. Not one that can't hold onto a job. Someone good. Everette, you had better do as I tell you. I'm in no mood for you to be acting out like this. So much like your father...I wish I had drowned you as a babe."

"Thank you for the compliment. I think that's the first nice thing you've ever said to me." She tried to think what he was talking about. "I don't mind being thought of as taking after my father. Anything is better than becoming like you."

Elba was put in a police car. She was so angry right now she could just about find herself a gun and take them all out. The nerve of some people. And the man driving the car wouldn't answer a single one of her questions. These people were hoodlums, every one of them.

~~~

"Mayor? There are two officers here to see you." It took him several seconds to realize they were talking to him. It might have been longer had Cassie not poked him in the side. "They said that they're here to talk to you about your mother."

"All right. Will you please see if they need anything? A room or some dinner? I don't know how long this will take, but I'd very much like them to be comfortable before they meet up with my mother." The man laughed then caught himself, changing it to a cough. "You know that there is no love lost between us, right? And even if I wasn't her son, I think I'd see humor in it as well."

"Yes, sir. She is...well, she's not a nice person, pardon me for saying so." Rett agreed and asked him to take care of the

112

men. When he was gone, he turned to Cassie.

"Well, Tart, are you ready for this?" She laughed at him. "My mother is a horrible person. I can't believe that I didn't notice it before now."

"I'm sure that you did, you just had blinders on because she's your mom." He nodded and held her to his body. It was just what he needed. "We have to see to my father after this. I'm sure he's not going to be any better. Maybe we can put them in the same cell together and she'll browbeat him into leaving."

"Maybe we can just run away and let everyone else sort this out." She said that wouldn't work, her dad could find her. "I guess. But when this is done, I want you to go away with me. Someplace quiet, without parents."

"Deal." He had wondered how he was going to propose to her. He'd gotten the ring a few days ago, and thought this was the best time ever. Letting her go, he went down on one knee and kissed her left hand. "What are you doing?"

"Proposing. Now hush while I do it." She laughed and told him it wasn't necessary. "It is to me. Now, keep quiet while I do this. Casandra Harmon, I love you more than I have ever thought possible to love someone else. You're the best thing that has ever happened to me. Even though you're a tart, according to some sources."

"Well, I guess it's better than being ungrateful, though I love you anyway." He kissed her finger before sliding the ring over her first knuckle. "Rett, you really don't have to do this."

"Ah, but I do. Casandra Harmon, will you do me the honor of becoming my wife? Being beside me forever? Loving me no matter how strange I become? Will you stay by my side through thick and thin? Laugh with me and have my children?" He slid the ring up to her hand, kissing it again before turning the ring so that she could see the design. "I found this one day while I was out walking the land around Danburn's house. I showed it to him later and he said that the earth had gifted it to me to give you. I had to have him explain that to me, how the two of you are as much a part of the earth as the soil is."

"We are. Him more so than me." He nodded and looked up at her. "You're waiting on me to answer, aren't you?"

"Well, it would help me to know if we're going to celebrate or not."

She got down on her knees in front of him. "This is in the tradition of my kind. Everette Welsh, I give to you all that I am, all that I can ever be. My dragon will protect you like no one ever will. From this day forward, I will love you forever. Be by your side when you need me, in front of you when you need that as well. I am your mate, as you are mine. We are one, we are dragon."

He kissed her then, feeling a connection like he'd never felt before. And when she told him she loved him, he did it again, knowing that for as long as they both were of this earth, no one would ever part them.

They were to talk with her father soon. It wasn't going to be an easy conversation, nor would it be all that friendly. But after dealing with his mom, Rett actually felt like he could handle him. Sort of. He was a dragon, after all.

Danburn had given him a heads up on what might happen once they were in the same room, but he'd not told Cassie yet. Rett was sure that whatever happened that day, it would not go well for any of them. Arlington Harmon wasn't going to be happy about the way his daughter was going to talk to him, nor the fact that she had a mate now. It was a game changer as far as him being able to rule her.

"She has strength now that she didn't before." Rett had asked Danburn what he meant. "With a mate, you, she no longer has to bow before him. There will be no compulsion strong enough that he can use on her that will make her bow before him. With you there, as her mate, her father will have no control over her. You either."

"You think he could have?" Danburn said he was sure of it. "But I'm not a dragon. I mean, for all intents and purposes, I'm just a human."

"Not any more you're not." Again, he asked what he meant. "You and her exchanged blood, correct?"

"Yes. I mean, it was just a little. She bit me the other day during…she bit me." Danburn nodded. "And I thought it would be wonderful if I did the same to her. Well, it was sexy and all, but I doubt it would have changed me."

"Our kind, we can't convert people like other paranormals can. But I will tell you that any children that you have, they'll be dragon, or mostly so. But you, you'll stay just as you are now, but no longer just a human. You'll have the same benefits she does. Healing quickly. Never getting ill. Infections will still harm you, both of you as a matter of fact, but you won't be able to die like you could before. And you are immortal."

"Okay, I get all that. What does this have to do with her father and his making us do what he wants? Surely he doesn't think he can make her do anything now. Unless he doesn't know about me." Danburn just smiled. "You didn't tell him, did you?"

"I saw no reason to let him think that she'd found her mate. It might be kind of fun for the two of you to show up and surprise him." Rett asked if he thought it would go over well. "Not on your life. He's going to not just be pissed off, but let his dragon go and try and harm you. He won't, but he might try."

"You mean that he'll attempt to burn me up?" Danburn said he might, but he'd never be able to. "And you're sure about this? I mean, totally and completely sure that he can't fry me where I stand?"

"Yes. I'm as sure of that as I am my love for Kendrick." It was as good as it got, and he knew that. "And if you want, I can be close enough to take care of him. Not that I think you'll need me, but I'll be there."

"If you think we can handle it, then I believe you. But I don't understand why you think he can no longer harm me." Danburn laughed. "I don't think I like you overly much right now."

"He can't hurt you because if he tries, Cassie will protect you like a momma bear would her cubs. He might not be able to die, but he surely will wish it if she gets the chance to take him on." Rett asked if she could kill her father. "No, I don't think so, but she will hurt him, enough that I'll have to step in. And I, my friend, can kill him. Easily."

Rett told Cassie what Danburn had said. "He's not happy about the money and jewels, I guess. Danburn interceded on my behalf before I met you. I not only got the money that belonged to me, but also things that were my mom's he had told me he got rid of. I think that Kendrick made him tell her

116

where they were hidden, and then Danburn got them for me. I have no idea why they'd go to so much trouble on my behalf, but I'm glad they did."

They were headed there now. The house that her father had rented wasn't far from the downtown area, so they walked. She told him some of the things that had been happening since her father decided that what was hers was his.

"I was surprised that he'd given it up so easily. Well, not easily, but that he'd not come after me when Danburn made him give it over." Rett asked her if he was able to do that to dragons. "Yes. Danburn is the oldest, and probably strongest, ever born. He is a dragon of the earth. Which means not only can he control the elements like me, but he also can move mountains. Literally."

"I heard that he formed the castle from the mountain. Is that true?" Cassie laughed. "I guess not then."

"No, Danburn did. Not only that, but he also formed the mountain and lake that he swims in, as well as gave it life. The legend says that not only was the land here barren when he arrived, but almost dead. He asked the earth for a place to keep his family safe and she obliged." Rett paused in his walk and she turned to look at him. "You don't believe me."

"I do. I think that's what has me so...I was going to say confused, but it's more than that. I'm in awe of him as well. To think.... When I went to him about the ring, he said that he thought there were a great many treasures in the belly of his lady. I thought he meant something else. But he meant the belly of the lady earth, didn't he?"

"More than likely. He talks to her all the time, I guess. And his dragon does as well." Rett asked her what she meant.

117

"When we were at the shelter, he asked if mine spoke to me. She doesn't, but his does, like they're two different people. It's another part of the legend that I heard. That he is two beings wrapped in one man."

"And Kendrick, she's his queen." Cassie said that she was. "And even though she cannot change into a dragon, she can command them."

"Yes. I think, no matter if she had met Danburn or not, she would have been able to do that. She was born to be the queen. I'm betting that they sort of called to each other. It's what I heard anyway."

He had a lot to think about. But he did know one thing... he wanted Danburn close when they got around to speaking to Arlington Harmon.

CHAPTER 8

Arlington wanted to go to the home and confront his errant child. The nerve of her going above his head like she had. Danburn, the English lord, had no more right to order him about than his child did making demands. He was going to see to that as well.

He looked over his treasures, the few that there were, and wondered briefly how he was going to get more. "I shall kill for it, that is what I shall do." His laughter rang through the big empty vault he was sitting in.

Two days ago he'd been called home. He didn't want to leave his daughter unattended, but there was no hope for it. There were things going on at his castle that needed his attention. And if nothing else, Arlington knew no one could take care of things the way he did. His way was death to those that bothered to disagree with him. And failing that, he would ruin them.

"My Lord, there are rebels outside. They wish a word with you." Arlington turned to his man at arms. "They wish that you would come to greet them."

"Do they really think me that naive? That I would leave

the walls of my home to go and greet them?" The man said nothing, not that he expected him to. "Tell them to go home, there is no reason for this trouble unless they wish to die today."

"I will, My Lord." When he didn't move, Arlington waited. So much was going on right now, though nothing that he wanted to deal with. "There is a matter of the bank, My Lord."

"The bank? I don't have anything to do with that institution. What is it they want?" The man, whose name Arlington neither knew nor cared to learn, handed him a sheet of paper. "Read it to me."

He couldn't read it for himself. He supposed he might have been able to figure it out after a time, but he'd long since given up on learning much more than his name when he saw it, and how to write it out when necessary. Really, to him it was a bunch of scribbles, but people thought it was his signature.

"It is a collection notice. They wish for you to pay your taxes. It claims that you are in arrears for a great deal." Arlington snatched the paper from him. "You have ten days to pay the outstanding amount or they will take your lands."

"What is the meaning of this? Of course I'm not going to pay them money. I refuse to pay taxes on land that has been in my family for more years than they have been in the banking business. Where do they get off thinking that a man such as myself should have to pay for land that I own?" The man said that he did not know, but that was what the paper said. "And does this paper say what amount they think to get from me?"

"Eleven million, seven hundred thousand, six hundred forty-nine dollars and seventeen cents, my lord." Arlington asked him to repeat himself. When he did, the man cleared his throat before continuing. "They say that you have not paid in over two decades, and with the penalties you will have to pay that amount to be caught up for this year. They will assess you for the next year when you are current."

"Why was I not informed of this sooner?" The man only nodded to the desk that was covered in unopened envelopes and other sundry. "Someone should have told me. Not that I have any intentions of paying such an amount, but I think it is remiss in them waiting this long in telling me."

"They claim, sir, that you have been notified more than most. I myself have asked them the same question, and their answer was that you should have returned at least one of their calls." Arlington threw the paper in the general direction of the mess upon his desk. "Sir, there is more. The bank said that because of this matter there is no money for you to spend on household goods and supplies. We are broke until you can pay the taxes they claim that you owe them. Or make other arrangements."

"I have no need for supplies. If I want it, I shall just go and get it." The man shook his head. "Have you heard what I do with people who disagree with me? They not only lose their heads, but there is generally no body to find."

"I am sorry, sir, but there is the matter of the house lighting that has been shut off. As well as the payments that are necessary for the staff." He asked him who authorized payment to anyone that worked for him. "Your lady wife, My Lord. She made sure we were all paid so that we might have food at our homes."

"This house, all the lands around it, who do you think

owns it?" The man said nothing, which was good. Arlington was sure that he'd not have the correct answer. "I do. My child, she has done this. Taken all the funds that were to run this house after her mother passed away. That upstart, Danburn, he is also the cause of this. Well, I will not be treated this way. You tell them to release the funds necessary and have it brought to me. I'll make sure that everyone is paid what they are owed from now on."

"I have heard that you were out looking for her. Do you think perhaps that is not a good idea?" Arlington stood up and the man backed from him. "The only reason I ask, My Lord, is because it is said that Lord English is at her side."

"He lets a mere woman do his work and you fear him? A woman who is no more dragon than you are." The man had no answer, but he did look like he had plenty of questions. "A woman called here, told me that I was to release funds to my child. As if she were deserving of them. Then when she was finished, she informed me that I was to come to the English castle and pay homage to her mate. Like I was going to do that on her say so."

The man only stared at him still. After dismissing him, Arlington locked the door behind him. He wanted no one to interrupt him for a few moments, time that he needed to plan his attack. And he would too. He had the right to demand that English give over his child and the monies that he so willingly parted with on the whim of a woman. There were things in the items that he gave to this man that he wanted returned. Arlington wanted it all, but the crown that had been his when his wife was alive, belonged to him.

The woman, the English mate, had made him release the

funds he'd had. There was no doubt in him that she'd used some sort of magic to make him do so. It was the fact that he'd willingly parted with not just the money, but the jewels as well. It had to be the work of magic that had made him do what he normally would not. She might not be a dragon, but there was something powerful about her.

English was a man that Arlington knew very little about. He was a great man, or so he'd been told. And an honest one. Which, as far as Arlington had ever known, would only get you into pitfalls that you couldn't escape. And Arlington would know all about those.

He looked over at his desk and wondered why no one had taken the time to clean that particular area of the castle. He laughed then, because he'd told them to leave this room the way he left it. It was the only way he was assured of keeping his secrets. Not that he had a great many of those left. His daughter had taken them from him as well.

Arlington knew the ways of his kind. He thought he should know them better than most. His own wife had been there when they were adopted, helping write laws and codes that would eventually kill off their kind in his opinion. Then she'd gone and made it so he couldn't change stuff around. What right did a female, of all people, have to do something like that?

On plenty of occasions they had argued bitterly about these rules. The law that he hated in particular was the one stating that he must, under all circumstances, remain true to his mate. Well, all mates must, but he thought that he should have been given a pass from such a stupid rule. He was Arlington, after all.

And because of this arguing over something that he'd not had a thing to do with, his wife had died. He'd not meant to poison her. Not really. What he'd wanted to do was make her ill enough that she would have to sign over all duties to him. Then he was going to change the laws that governed their kind, something that would suit him and his fellow dragons. She had died, he knew, knowing his plan all along.

Pulling out the book that had been in his offices since he'd been a newly widowed dragon, he looked over the rules there. And there were plenty of them to see. Not that he could read any, but he knew them word for word. Some his wife had quoted on the very day she'd died, telling him, with her own voice, that he was doomed to die by his own stupidity.

"And how does this happen? I have no more intentions of taking my own life than you do to kill your child. That is such nonsense." She only rolled to her back, her body too thin, her dragon so weak and unable to come out from lack of food due to the high fevers. "Why do you not just sign over your control to me? I will carry on as you have."

"You have no intentions of doing any such thing, you monster. I know what you have done, Arlington. And according to law, you will get your comeuppance soon enough. Not by my hand, but that of your child." He laughed. A daughter would harm him? Not likely. "You'll see, Arlington. And when she does this for me, I will be here waiting for you with open arms."

"Open arms?" She nodded and said that she'd have a blade in each hand to run him through when he came to her. "Then I shall not come to you. I will avoid you for all time."

Two hours later, she was dead.

Arlington had dismissed all that had attended her, telling them he wished to be alone with his wife. But what he wanted to do, and did, was dance. A joyful jig that no one would understand but him. He was free to do as he pleased. And the first thing he wanted to do was change the laws. But he could not. He hadn't gotten the permission from her before she died.

And now he had been called to her family home to deal with the banks. Banks? Who needed them in the first place? Certainly not him. And now it seemed that because of his lack of planning before his wife died, he might lose it all because of his child. Casandra was going to have to pay.

"She will need to die. Without an issue from her body, nor a mate to plant one, she cannot do anything but what I tell her. And once she is dead, I will be the only one left that can change the laws." It was why he'd been searching for her for so long, to kill her. "Then when the laws are the way I want them, I will deal with this banking order once and for all."

He made arrangements to go back to where she was staying. There were things happening that would change only when he was in charge. Arlington was going to not just deal with the bank, but everyone that had done anything to him since he'd been able to kill off his wife. And he would do the same to his child too. The nerve of his wife, not giving him a son so that he could make him in the image of himself. He was going to have a great deal of fun despite it.

"I shall burn the bank to the ground with everyone in it." He loved that idea as he got into his limo. Arlington thought that he'd make it a rule for all dragons, to burn all banks to the ground with the employees inside.

~~~

Elba was going to see her boy today. At least he'd better be here. And as soon as she had him under her rule again, she was going to demand he take care of things. Like her clothing. There was no reason that she should be subjected to wearing such a thing as a cheap orange jumpsuit. Not only was it unbecoming, but she was sure that there had been a hundred-other people wearing it before her.

"You tell them to release me this moment." He asked her why she'd think he'd do that for her. "Because I demand it. And I'm your mother, much to my shame. I will not conduct this conversation with you while I'm chained like an animal."

He shrugged and stood up. When she asked him what he was doing, he told her. "I'm leaving. You won't talk when chained like you are, and I have no desire to spend any time here without you being in them. You're not a nice person."

"Oh, I'm not? Well, good. Nice people are saps, and you are the biggest one I know." He just smiled at her and Elba wanted to snatch him bald. He was going to have a lot to make up for when she was released from this godforsaken place. "What have you done to yourself anyway? You dress up to come see me in that cheap suit to impress me somehow? Well, I have news for you, you're not all that impressive even in that."

"As a matter of fact, this wasn't cheap, but I thank you for noticing it. And I have no desire to impress you at all. In fact, I couldn't care less what you think of me. The only reason I'm here is because they said that they can't get you to understand why you've been arrested. I told them you knew, but you didn't care for it so you weren't going to listen. It's been that way your whole life, hasn't it? Something doesn't jive with your way of thinking so you ignore it." She asked him what he was talking about. "You. And your own set of guidelines that you expect everyone to follow. But it won't work with me. Not anymore. You killed those people and blamed it on Dad."

"I did no such thing." She reached for her cane, the one that had been taken from her as soon as she arrived, and was angry it wasn't there for her to use. "Is that what he told you? That I was driving? Lies, all of it. Why have you been listening to such a thing? I told you, several times, to stay away from him. He is dead to you."

"Dad told me all about it. He said a great many things, as a matter of fact." That man was going to have to straighten up or she'd make him regret opening his mouth. "He said that not only were you driving that night, but that he'd not even been in the car. You'd tossed him out of it when he disagreed with the way you were raising me."

"He was such a fool when it came to you. Thinking that I was too hard on you. Cruel is what he called me. I was no crueler to you then than I am now. You would have turned out much better had you just been beaten more." She waited for him to argue with her as well, but all he did was sit there, staring at her as if he had not a care in the world. "Don't you have anything to say for yourself? Don't you want to disagree with me? That's what he did. All the time. And it turns out I was right, as usual."

"Arguing with you is a waste of time." She told him she was glad he finally got that into his head. "In fact, Mother dear, I'm never going to argue with you again."

There was something going on. She had no idea what, but he was just too nice to her about all this. Elba wasn't a fool; he was trying to get her to do something for him. He was just like his father in that. Well, he'd find out soon enough that she did nothing for anyone unless it was in her favor.

"What have you done about finding me a lawyer? I need a good one. Someone that knows which end is up." He told her he was an attorney. "Yes, I suppose you might be, but I need one that is good. You're not and never will be. I don't care about the cost either. You can decide together however you want to pay him. But I want out of here, Everette. Today if you think you can manage that."

"No." She asked him what he meant. "I'm not going to pay someone to represent you. I'm not going to call anyone for you, and I most certainly will not get you out of here. In fact, you should know that I like you being where I know you're not plotting against people, nor hurting them. As I've pointed out several times now, you aren't nice. In fact, I think you're a bitch."

"If I had my cane you'd see what sort of person I am. Don't use that sort of language around me, Everette. I will not tolerate it. And what makes you think I'm not plotting, as you call it? I do not; I make things right. Regardless, get me out of here, Everette. I have no more reason than you to be in here." He told her she'd killed two people. "I most certainly did not. Your father all but confessed to it. And him being in prison suited me just fine. I like myself and enjoy my own company. You and your father never got that."

"Oh, I think we understood it just fine. As for him confessing, he didn't. Dad's been claiming he's innocent all along. The really sad part is, he never gave you up until recently. Also, and this is what pisses me off the most, you told him that I hated him. Which I do not." She told him again that she didn't care for his language nor his tone. "I don't give a fuck what you think about me or what I say."

When he stood up, she had a feeling that not one thing she told him to do was going to be done. Asking him about the lawyer, he told her again that he wasn't doing it. She wanted to hit him, smack him upside the head and make him do it. But chained like she was, she couldn't even wipe her nose should she want to.

"I'm not going to sit here and stand for this. You'll do as you're told or so help me, Everette, I will make your life a living hell." He told her that she'd already done that. "Then you should know that I can do much more to you."

"You mean like take my father from me when there was no reason for it? How about lie to me for years about your innocence? Not that I really believed you were, but about the murder of those people I did. Or how you took my hard earned money when you didn't have to?" Elba started to tell him that he owed her. "And if you bring up that old story about how I owed you, then you're dead wrong about that. Whatever you think I did has long since been paid in full."

"I'm your mother, much to my shame. You'll take care of me as I see fit. And I want out of here. I don't belong in jail." He said that she didn't. "Good. Now, I want these cuffs taken off as well. I want—"

"You don't deserve to be in here because you should be in prison, rotting away like you wanted my dad to. But have you ever noticed how it's always what you want? What you

129

demand? I'm over that, and you." Elba opened her mouth but he interrupted her again. "I won't be back. I have a lot of years to make up for with my dad, and I have a fiancée too."

"Fiancée? You found some fool to marry you? I did not think you'd ever get anyone to spread their legs for you, much less marry you." She laughed. It was too funny, his joke about a wife. "I suppose you'll be having children with this woman too? Perhaps bring them by to see their old grandma?"

"Never." There was a hardness in his voice that startled her. A finality that she'd never heard in her entire life. "My children will know of you, perhaps. But they will never see you. Never send you cards at holidays, nor will they ever refer to you as anything but the murderous woman that you are."

"I don't know why you'd talk to me that way, but it's good they won't come by. I'm not nearly old enough to be a grandmother anyway. Especially to brats that you might spawn." He laughed at her. "I don't think you'll be laughing so hard, Everette, when I tell them what sort of person you really are."

"You're well old enough to be a grandmother. At sixty-four I would think that you're closer to being a great grandma, wouldn't you?" She told him she wasn't that old. "But you are, aren't you? You had me late in life, thirty-five. I saw my birth certificate when I was going through that mausoleum you call a home."

Her temper burned through her like a hot volcanic flame... she even felt it heat her face. Had she been able to stand or even reach him, she would have hurt him badly, perhaps even put him in the same situation she was, without use of her leg. And even though hers was only temporary, his would not be.

"What were you doing in my house? I never gave you permission to go through my things." He laughed again and made his way to the door. "Everette, so help me, if you do not get me a good attorney, I'm going to make you regret it. And you know that I'm aware of all your secrets."

"Do you? I don't think so. But I know yours now, don't I?" She wondered what he might have found, what sort of information he had on her. Or thought he had. "I've found out a great deal lately. And the money that you have stashed all over the house as well."

"That's mine." He only shook his head at her. "What would you do with it but to spend it on whores and drugs? What about that tart I saw you with? Is she using my money?"

"My soon-to-be-wife is putting it to good use." She told him he wasn't married. "As a matter of fact we are. And as soon as we can, we're going to have children. None of which you'll be able to corrupt."

"You think that's ever going to happen?" She laughed, and even to her it sounded bitter and cold. "You can't get anyone pregnant, Everette. You want to know why? Because you're a worthless human being, just like your father is. And do you want to know something else? He thinks you're his child, but you are not. You are a product of a man who meant no more to me than you do."

Elba wanted to see him squirm. To be angry and lash out at her. It would do her heart good to see him lose his temper, to drop the façade of acting better than her. But when he just stood there, staring at her with a small smile on his face, she thought perhaps he'd not heard her. But his next words confirmed that he had.

"He's known since my fifth birthday that I wasn't his son. He told me." She watched his face, just to see if he was bluffing. "When I broke my arm falling down the stairs when you pushed me, he had me tested. He's known since then. And the really wonderful part of it is, it didn't matter to him. Dad said that having me there during his life with you made things better."

Elba was moving back to her cell when she realized that Everette hadn't done anything that she told him to do. Her thoughts, all of them ways to get back at the two of them, were circling around in her head quickly and without any sort of order.

First and foremost, her husband knew about her boy and he hadn't said a word. George was a fool. A bigger chump than she'd ever thought him to be. He'd known that the bastard child that she'd pawned off on him wasn't his child, yet he continued to treat it like his own. "What a fool he is."

CHAPTER 9

Cassie wasn't sure if she should have been thrilled by her new job or scared out of her mind. Both she supposed. Running the shelter all on her own now was a job that she'd never had before, yet it was a great deal like many that she'd done. The list of things she'd have to do was easy, so long as she had the right people, she supposed.

Make sure that the people were happy. She could do that, now that she didn't have her hands tie. She supposed that she hadn't really. Had Cassie asked, she could have done a lot of things for the people in her care. And the fact that Lord Danburn felt she could do this well made her feel like she was on top of the world.

She looked behind her when she heard her name. Elissa, Danburn's mom, and Kendrick were coming down the long hall. They were talking to each other, both waving their hands, speaking quickly and seemingly having a good time. When she was about to go to them, a man she'd seen around the building stepped in front of her.

"I was wondering if you could assist me with something." She looked at him, wondering where she'd see him before.

133

She couldn't place his accent, but she was sure she knew him. Cassie asked him how she could help him. "I'm hungry, and was wondering if you could show me where the dining area is. I'm a little lost."

"There is plenty of food here should you need it, and there are signs to show you where to go. Also, facilities should you need to bathe. If you need one, there is a doctor on staff today. But for now, we're not open for anyone stay over. I'm sorry." He grinned at her, but she still had a feeling that she knew him from somewhere.

"You have a great deal of help here. I mean, I didn't expect you to have so many people just hanging around. Did you?" She nodded, not quite sure what he was talking about. "They don't all look like they're homeless. Some of them, a lot as a matter of fact, aren't even human. You'd think that they were trying to protect you or something."

"Protect? I'm not sure what you're implying, but these are my friends." He nodded, still staring at her. "You should really go now. I don't think there is anything that we can do for you."

"Ah, but you can." He looked to her right, and she knew that he was seeing both the other women. "You ladies have other things to do? Casandra and I were just having a nice conversation here."

"No, not particularly...we're here for Cassie. You, however, I think were asked to go." He frowned, and she knew that his compulsion wasn't doing what he wanted on Kendrick or Elissa. Kendrick laughed then, talking to the man again. "If you don't leave now, you're going to be in a world of hurt. I think whatever it is you have in mind for us, isn't going to work."

"I have no idea what you're talking about." His accent was gone now, either anger or the fact that he'd never had one making him speak perfect English. "I only asked for a room and a place to lay my head."

"Who sent you and why? Because men who wear four thousand dollar suits and expensive shoes no more need a place to lay their heads than I do." The man struggled. Cassie thought for sure he wasn't going to answer her. But when Kendrick asked him again, putting more force in her voice, he finally gave in.

"Arlington. He said that I was to get her free of this place and he would do the rest." He dropped to his knees, his nose, eyes, and ears bleeding. "I work for him on occasion and he pays me well. What are you doing to me?"

Cassie looked at Kendrick. "Let him go. He's told you what you wanted. Let him go." She was already shaking her head. "Please. I don't think he should be killed for this, do you?"

"I'm not doing this. I asked, he answered. The rest of this, the bleeding, that's not me." Kendrick looked at Elissa, who said it wasn't her either. "I don't know what is making him—"

Before she could complete her statement the man fell to his side. Blood was pouring from him now. Not just his nose, but even his skin seemed to have sprouted some kind of bloody leak.

Cassie dropped to her knees beside him, and he rolled over and looked up at her. She could see the pain there. The magic too. Before she could touch him to help, he told her no.

"Don't touch me. I think…he's poisoned me because I

could not make you do as I wanted. You will die if you touch me." She nodded, feeling helpless. "I owed him. Not money — that would have been easy to repay — but for something else. You mustn't let him take you."

"What does he want? Besides my death?" He screamed then. She knew that he was hurting and started to rise when he said her name softly.

"There is a book, the book of rules. Your mother, she wrote it. He cannot change it without your death. He wishes things to be his way." She didn't know what he was talking about, but she thought that Elissa did. She leaned over the man then, her face a study in worry.

"Does he have it? Have you seen the book?" He nodded, his body gripped in pain again. "Where? Where is it? His home? The one he shared with his mate?"

"Yes." The scream hurt her ears. The man bent in half, his back breaking when he did. Cassie stood and stepped back from him. There was nothing anyone could do for him now. "Don't let him get you." Then he was dead.

None of them moved. Cassie wasn't sure what was going on, but one thing was clear...her father was going to try and kill her. For a book. One that she had no knowledge of.

"You have questions." Cassie nodded at Elissa. "I do as well. But if you could hold off for a little while, I have things I need to find out first. Like if he's correct in your death giving him the rights."

"Rights to change the rules." Elissa nodded. "I.... Will he really need for me to be dead for this to work? I mean for him to do this, whatever it is?"

"I don't know." Cassie nodded and looked back at the

dead man. "He saved you. I don't know why, but I'm glad that he did."

"So am I, even if I don't understand it." Elissa said she'd be back and left them there. Cassie looked at Kendrick. "I need help. Protection and a great deal of it. Rett will as well. His mother too I guess, even though I think he's written her off."

"Done. I would ask that you take on a few more people in your home. Ones that can work, yet also help if you need it." Cassie nodded. "He won't get you, Cassie. We'll assist you so he doesn't."

"He sent a man here to kill me. Or maybe not kill, but to take me to him. I can only assume that he was going to do the deed." Kendrick said that would be her assumption as well. "All sorts of thoughts are running through my head right now. Like...he's not a nice person, I knew that, but he wanted me dead."

"Go and find Rett. Tell him what's going on and then stay with him today. I can take care of this place for a few hours." She wanted to tell Kendrick that she'd be all right, but honestly, she was overwhelmed. "You should also call on Shawn. He can be places that we can't."

She decided that was a good idea as well. But instead of calling or reaching, she decided to talk to him face to face. He might be busy or something, but she needed to see him when she explained.

Once she made it to the edge of the township line, he was waiting for her, it seemed.

"A man just tried to kill me." He nodded, his wolf as black as the dark woods behind him. "He was sent by my father."

We're connected, you and I. Would you prefer that I come to

137

you as I am now or as a man? She told him man and he shifted quickly. "There are two more such men in this town. One we have been keeping an eye on for Lord Danburn. The other, I believe he is with your father as well. He is a man who has a great deal of blood upon his hands."

"While walking here, I had a thought. Did he kill my mother?" He said nothing. "Yeah, I thought so. She died of an infection, he told me. But I think it was more. Maybe even whatever he did to the man he sent for me."

"I could tell, should you know where she is buried. I can smell things, small essences that few others can. But you should be aware that I will easily take his life and that of any other person who has threatened you. You only have to say the word." She told him where her mother's marker was. "I will take care of this for you, but you must allow me to have my men near you at all times. Your father being a dragon could harm them, but others that he may send would not."

"I was going to ask you about that. Thank you. Also, Rett. He's immortal, but he could still get to me through him. All I can think of right now is that he tried to kill me." He watched her. She supposed someone should. Cassie felt like she was on the edge of something, a great mountain or even a deep ocean, and she was just a small push from falling in. "Elissa is going to find out some information for me. Something about a book. Do you know what that might be?"

"A book of dragons, or something more?" She told him what the man had said. "I would imagine there is such a book. One of rules that someone would have put together. There is for my kind. And like your mother, I had a hand in writing it as well. But if what you say is true, that he can only change things when you're dead, I would think that there is more to the spell than that. A loophole, so to speak."

"How will I know what that is?" He said that Elissa would. "I guess. She's older than even my father. What do you think he wants to change? I mean, the rules have been working for a long time. What would he find that he doesn't like in them?"

"A man such as your father, he would want them to benefit him. There must be some rule in it that keeps him from this. What is it that your father treasures over all else?" She told him. "Money and power go hand in hand when it comes to magic. If there is a rule in the book, one let's say that makes it so he cannot ever oversee money—like everyone's—he'd want that changed, don't you think?"

She had no idea what was in the book, so she had no way of thinking what he'd want to change. Shawn told her that he had sent a great many of his pack to watch over Rett. He also said that several were going to be wandering their land, as well as Danburn's and the shelter. Thanking him, she started to leave, then turned back. There was one more thing she needed to know.

"The man that was killed, he said that my father poisoned him. That had I touched him, I more than likely would have died as well. What sort of magic, besides black, would do that? I mean, is it a casting spell, or one that he would have to put in the man?" Shawn asked her why that was important. "Because I know a few witches that can help me out if it's a casting one. Sort of give him a taste of his own blackness."

"I would say that the man was a dead one even before he saw you. And that your father figured that you'd disobey this man and not do what he wanted. So he killed the man, hoping

139

that on some level you'd feel obligated to help him when he fell ill." She nodded, thinking he was right. "There was to be contact, he thought, before you could get whatever he had within, correct?"

"Yes. He told me not to touch him." Shawn grinned. "So it's an actual poison that this man ingested and it killed him. Contact poison."

"You are very brilliant, Cassie. I don't think your sire is aware of that or he might have left you alone." She asked him what he meant. "I can see that you are thinking of ways to take him out before he does you, are you not? If so, your father has it in his head that you are a.... Well, I was going to say sap, but I think he believes you to be nothing more than an empty headed female that would go blindly into a situation. And he poisoned this man, just in the event that you had help from someone else."

"He thinks women are useless. Only good for one thing." Shawn nodded as they made their way back to town. "I might have been too, going blindly where he wanted me, had I not met Rett and Danburn."

"Your father is a man without trust." She asked him again what he meant. "A man who cannot trust others, or in this case, that whatever is told to him is the truth. No matter how glaringly true it is. That alone will be his downfall. He will believe, with all that he is, that you are still subject to his rule. And the fact that you have matured, gotten a mate, and had good things happen to you will not factor into his need or desire to have you do what he wants. He will die because of that."

Cassie nodded. It was true, all of it. It was as if Shawn

knew her father as well as she did. And he was going to have to die, there was no hope for it. She only hoped that she could do it before he hurt one of the others, namely Rett.

~~~

Rett knew something was wrong, but he had asked Cassie several times what it was and all she'd said to him each time was that she was working on it. He wasn't sure if it because she didn't think he could help, or she really was working on it. Rett looked at Elissa when she cleared her throat. Everyone at the table paused in what they were eating and turned to look at her.

"I've had several of the people that work for me looking into things. And I've gone over notes that my late husband would pore over for hours. The Book of Dragon has been around longer than most trees in the forest, even before this castle sat here." Danburn asked her how she knew. "Because my mother, your grandmother, helped adopt it. She was there, like so many others were in the beginning, making a way for us all to get along without troubling the humans of our time."

"My father has it." Elissa turned to Cassie. "And what that man said today is true. He wants to be able to change it to suit himself."

"Yes. There was a spell put upon the book when it was deemed finished. I knew that my mother was one of the people that thought a spell was necessary. If not, then anyone who held the book and all that was written in it could easily have turned the tables to get everything he desired. Such as what your father is doing." Danburn asked why the holder was able to change the book. "He can't. Not until his daughter is dead."

Rett had heard about the man today, and been so afraid that he'd gone to find Cassie to make sure she was all right. Not that he understood what had happened, he just knew that she'd been threatened.

"I don't understand. He has to kill his daughter to be able to change the laws in a book that is older than Danburn? Why not just cross out the ones that piss him off and be done with it?" Rett was sure there was more to it than that, but as he was the youngest person in the room by far with the exception of Kendrick, he had no idea how things worked a long time ago. "I'm sorry. I just want to understand."

"And you should. Long ago, there were nine of them. Dragons of some wealth, and a great deal of power. Lady Windburg, Allison, was one of them. That would be Cassie's mother. My mother and her sister were two more. There were others, I know, but I cannot find their names. I think that too was on purpose. To keep them safe, and their families." Elissa smiled. "I'm sorry. I got off track. Anyway, these women, as all of them were by the way, gathered together to make these rules that all dragons, of any size or wealth, would follow. There were consequences too, but let me finish this first."

"Women. They're the ones that put this book together?" Elissa nodded at him. "Are they more powerful than their male counterparts?"

"No. It's just that, from what I could find, the men thought it to be women's work. For them to figure out the rules that would govern them. I think, from all I've been able to gather, they thought that they were only giving their wives busy work. I don't think any of them actually thought they'd do it." Elissa smiled. "My own mother was quite proud of what she'd done, and told my father it had been fun. So when it was finished, she along with the others decided it was perfect. And being so, Allison put a dragon spell upon it."

"Do you know the spell?" Elissa told Danburn that she did now. "And knowing this spell, does that mean you can change it? Alter it so that Arlington won't be able to have the power of it?"

"I cannot change it, no." She turned to Cassie. "Cassie is her daughter, the only blood relative of Allison, and the one that holds all the power. So, I'm happy to say, it falls to Cassie."

"But I don't have any magic in me." Rett laughed…it was funny that she thought that. When she turned to look at him, her face red, he kissed her. "What I meant to say is, I don't know how to use the sort of magic that my mom did to do this. I have some things that she passed on to me, but nothing on the scale that would make me think I could put a spell on something."

"Oh, but you can." Elissa sat down before Cassie. "You have a very special magic, don't you? One that you have kept to yourself, even from your father. The dragons."

"Dragons?" Cassie looked at Danburn when he asked. "You mean you can call dragons to you?"

"No, she has them. Six, correct?" Cassie nodded and reached for Rett's hand. Rett held her tightly as Elissa continued. "The gift of dragons, clones of herself, which do not only what she asks of them, but have powers of their own. According to the information I found, your mother used those dragons, hers, to bind the book to herself and you. No one can change that unless you are both gone. Then it falls to the next in line. Which would be your father."

"What sort of changes would he like to make?" Elissa said nothing, but Rett could tell that she knew the answer to Cassie's question. "You have to tell me. I need to know."

"He wishes to be the king of dragons. And that would afford him all the riches attached with the title. Homage would be paid to him. Women would be given to him in lieu of some misdeed. He would have a castle too, whatever one that he deems perfect." Cassie asked her how much more. "He could kill anyone that he wishes, any dragon that comes to challenge him would never win as he would have all the power."

"He'd take this castle, wouldn't he? And kill Danburn and you." She nodded at Rett's quiet question. "There would be no stopping him. Anything that he disagreed with, he'd simply change it to suit him."

"Yes. Magic too. The same that holds him from the book, it would be his. Powerful witches would owe him. Creatures of the earth, faeries, brownies, all of them would have to bow before him."

"Can I stop him?" Elissa nodded at Cassie. "You know how? Is there some sort of spell that I can use to keep him from taking everything from everyone?"

"You must kill him, with your dragons, before he kills you. And he will should you find yourself in his clutches." Cassie got up to pace the room. Elissa looked at Rett. "Arlington will take you next, or try to. He might not have known about you before, but he will soon enough. Because of this attempt that failed, he'll look into her life to see why she didn't do as he wished. He'll find you, and if he gets you, he'll kill you both."

144

"Because I love her." Elissa nodded and smiled. "Can I be kept from him? I mean, is there a way for me to not fall to his power?"

"Oh yes. I'm not sure how you're going to like it, but there is a way." He told her he'd do anything, whatever it took. "You have to let her dragons take your life."

Rett wasn't sure how that was to work. If the dragons killed him, then he'd be dead. He could hear her explain it to him, saying things his mind couldn't wrap around. It wasn't until he felt the sting of someone hitting him that he was able to focus on something other than his death. He looked into the face of Danburn.

"You ready to listen now?" Rett said nothing, but nodded. "No, I don't think so. You're still not listening, just thinking too hard. I'll speak, you'll listen to me for a bit."

"I have to die." Danburn shook his head. "She said that I had to let her dragons take my life. I'm pretty sure that means I have to die."

"No, she said that they had to take your life, she did not say that you had to die." He was more confused than before. "Have you seen them? The dragons?"

"Yes. They're about a foot tall, in varying shades of green. Dark to light I guess. Fast too. What does that matter? They're fucking big enough to kill me, I think." Danburn laughed. "You know, I don't think I like you overly much right now."

"The dragons have to take you." Rett exhaled loudly. "Let me explain. They have to take you by running through you."

"And that's not going to kill me? I see. They have these special powers that when they run though a person, they not only don't die but they're magical." Danburn nodded. "I was

145

making a joke."

"It's what has to be done. They have to run through your body fast and hot. It will hurt, I guess, but you won't die. The reason is because you're her mate. And when they leave your body, quicker than you can blink, not only will they leave a part of their magic behind, but they will give you a sort of armor too." He stared hard at him, not fully understanding. "You've seen them, correct? You know that they're a part of her, a split of her."

"I'm confused. Just tell me what I have to do." He told him to stand up. "And that's going to help you tell me how?"

He saw them then, the dragons. They were standing across the room from him, breathing fire but not burning anything. Rett had a feeling that he should have been paying more attention when the first one hit him in the belly.

The heat burned his entire body. Rett was sick with it. Before he could beg for it to stop, the second dragon hit him, burning into him through his throat and neck. There was more after that, pain blurred with pain.

His body hurt from the inside out. Just as he was ready to drop, to let whatever was going on kill him, he felt arms wrap around him. Danburn. Danburn was holding him up so that they could finish him off. There wasn't any way to beg him to stop, to get Danburn to let him go. His throat was raw; he knew that his insides were hanging out. Blood had to be pouring from him, yet he was too afraid to look. Then it was as if someone had turned it off with a switch. Everything was fine.

Then he screamed. It felt like he'd been put into a vat of hot oil and was being cooked from the inside out. Rett knew that he'd been lied to…he was going to die.

Chapter 10

Arlington felt the earth tremble under his feet. Smiling, he wanted to howl to the world that he was king, that his man had done what he needed and he was lord. As he started for his throne room, to sit upon his chair and think about his plans, he was knocked down, his body a part of the earth.

It took him several tries to sit up. He was sick, his belly rebelling with even the slightest thoughts of food or water. When he was finally on his ass, his legs stretched out in front of him, he closed his eyes against the tilting of the earth, the way that things swayed back and forth too quickly.

Staggering to a standing position, he held onto the tree closest to him. Arlington stood there for several seconds before he leaned over to puke. There was little in his belly, but it was enough to make him sick yet again. As he stood there holding onto the tree, all he could think about was that he'd been poisoned.

It took him over an hour to get into his home. Sitting in his chair, he wasn't sure if he should hold his belly or head. Both were hurting him badly enough that he wanted to crawl into a hole and simply die. He was that sick.

149

The knock at his door had him shouting at them to go away. That made his head sicker, his belly rebel more. When the door opened he tried to sit up, but all he could do was groan and moan as the woman made her way into his office as if she owned it.

"You don't know me." He said that much was true. "Yes, I guess it is. Funny how that happens. You have someone just barge into your life without so much as a handshake or a smile. I'm not referring to me, but to you on this."

"Who the hell are you?" She just grinned and looked around. "Get out of here. I don't have time for whatever it is you're selling. Unless of course it's yourself, then I might be persuaded."

"You know as well as I do that you're much too sick to even get it up, much less use it. Not that I would want to, but I'm thinking that you having any sort of pleasure with any sex is long gone." He asked her what she was talking about. "Your magic, it's gone."

He stared at her and knew that she was telling him the truth. He watched her carefully when she got up to walk around his office. There were things here, a great many of them, which she had no right to see. Not being a mere female that is. Before he could tell her again to get out, she plucked a book from the shelf and held it in her hands.

"Put that back. That is of no concern of yours." She pulled it to her chest and smiled again. "Are you addled? I said for you to put that back. Right now, before I come over there and make you."

"Have you figured it out yet? I mean, there are so many clues that you should be able to." He asked her what she was talking about. "The reason you're so sick. Why you've been feeling all the pains of a man your age. It's literally right here in front of you."

Arlington started to ask her again what she was talking about when he noticed the book she had in her hands. It was his book, the Book of Dragon. He stood up, staggered again, and held on to his desk until it passed. All the while she stood there grinning at him like some sort of halfwit.

The book's cover had been forged from the scale of a dragon. The hard coating that held the rules was a deep red, veined with other colors that were too numerous to discern. The lock, something that he'd just figured out how to breach, was made from the tooth of the same dragon that had given up the scales. His wife's.

It even held a few spells within it. All were written on parchment so fine that he doubted anyone, even with today's high tech, could ever repeat. The hands that wrote them, including his wife, were from now dead dragons. Women who had nothing better to do than to make life difficult for the men that had taken them to their beds.

"Have you figured it out yet? Do you know?" He growled low, hoping to frighten her enough that she'd run screaming from his presence. "You have no idea, do you? You think yourself poisoned, that this will pass. But it will not, Father dear. Not ever."

"Father? Who are you? What the fuck do you want coming here?" She laughed again and he knew it, had heard it less and less as the years had gone by, but it was the laugh of his Allison. "You're an impostor. Put the book back where you got it and get out now before I kill you."

"You cannot." She made her way back to the seat she'd been in before, his book still in her arms. "We'll talk, you and me. Or I will and you'll listen. There is plenty for us to discuss, don't you think?"

"What I think is that you'd better do as you're told or I'll show you what happens to people who piss me off." He was getting highly ticked off about the laughing. There was nothing, not one thing, funny about this. "Tell me who you are. I know you're not who you claim. My daughter is not so lovely, and she has the look of her mother too much to be considered even half pretty."

"Thank you. But I am your daughter, Casandra Allison Harmon. I've found my other half, so I guess it's also Welsh now." Arlington leaned heavily on the desk. "There, I think some of this is finally getting through to you. I'm your daughter, from your wife, Allison. Are you understanding now?"

"What are you doing here?" He sat down in his chair again, his legs too wobbly to hold him up, Not only from being ill, but what her being here meant. To his plans, to his life. All of it. "You have no right to be here. I want you to put my property back and get the hell out of here."

"No. As I mentioned, I have things to tell you. Did you kill her?" He knew who she spoke of, her mother, but he said nothing. He wasn't going to answer regardless how many times she asked. And he thought she would too. "No matter that you won't make claim that you did. I know the answer. Did you know that the poison you used, the odor of it, lingers for many years, decades even, afterward? You reek of it."

"I most certainly do not." He just admitted that he had

used it. Arlington knew that she thought herself clever, but he was much smarter. "There is no odor about me because I have not used any poisons."

Before he could blink, she was standing before him with his hand in hers. There on the palm was the long streak of poison, the very kind he'd used to kill her mother. Arlington snatched his hand away and put it under the desk as she made her way back to the chair.

He had known that there was a chance he'd be tainted by what he'd done. Grinding up the iron into a thick paste had been dangerous, but in order to serve it to Allison, put it in the tea that she drank every day, he was willing to take it. But he'd been so careful.

"With your magic depleting, you'll start to feel all your misdeeds. Like the time you were stabbed when robbing another man's estate. The time you fell from the wall of a house when you were nearly caught raping a woman. I'm sure that you'll feel that of—"

"What do you mean, rape? That word has no meaning to me." He snorted. "Rape indeed. A woman should enjoy spreading her legs for one such as myself. Do you know that I have had more women than any man or dragon ever has? It is my right, by law, that I am able to fuck who I please."

"And you have. Even if the women were unwilling." He just shook his head. There was no way he could explain this to a female. She would think all manner of things were wrong that he'd done. "As I was saying, you're going to start feeling a great deal more of your aches and pains. So much so that I think you'll wish you were dead."

"I will live forever." She said that was the point, for now.

He hated women, and this one was becoming particularly tiresome. "What is it you hope to do to me? And don't think I didn't notice that you still have my book. I want you to be gone from here, now as a matter of fact. I have many things I need to get done."

"The men you sent for me, they're both dead." He wondered what had become of them. No matter, he thought, he'd just have to hire someone else. "Any others that you send from now on, they'll meet the same fate. I'm asking you this one time…will you stop trying to kill me? It will no longer work."

"They weren't to kill you, daughter, but to bring you here so that I might do the job myself." He leaned back, trying to look as if he wasn't in excruciating pain. "I have a plan, you see, and you being alive the way you are, is messing it up. You should know that when you are dead, it will benefit me greatly. And is that not what you should want? For your father to be the greatest there is? To have the very best of everything?"

"You'd think that, wouldn't you?" He nodded, not sure of the tone she had right now. But when she stood, he did as well. "I'll be leaving you now, Father dear. You enjoy whatever is left of your life."

She was gone before he could move. His body was failing him and he had no idea why. He was sure that this mere female had done it, whatever it was. But he also knew that she wasn't smart, nor learned, enough to do anything that would harm him for long.

It took him the rest of the day to get to his bed. There were no servants around that he could get to come to his aid, no cane he could have walked with. Nothing save his own body.

And it was drenched in sweat one moment, then chilled to the bone the very next. He was sicker than he'd ever been, and he was going to make his daughter pay for whatever she'd done to him.

Pulling his cell phone out, something he'd only just learned to use, he pressed the buttons that would bring him help. Not in the form of domestic help — he still didn't understand where they were — but to get his daughter in line. It would happen today if he could manage it. As soon as the call was answered, he grinned. Things were going to go his way soon.

"Get her. Today. Or pay the price." He closed the connection and closed his eyes. It was as good as done as far as he was concerned. Arlington would be in the possession of not just his book, but the bloodletting to make him in charge.

~~~

Rett sat behind the prosecutor. He was there to make sure that justice was served. His father, now released, was sitting beside him. Rett was surprised at how much he'd aged in the last few years. His dad was looking very much his seventy years.

"She's not going to be happy about any of this." Rett told his dad he didn't care. "I don't think that's right either, son. She's your mother, after all."

"She is, but she's also a very evil, manipulative woman who killed someone, two people actually, and let you go to jail for it. Not to mention all the million and one things she's done since then." His dad nodded but didn't say anything else. "I'm glad you're out, Dad. We have a great deal to catch up on."

155

"I'm glad as well. I like that young bride of yours. She's a pistol. And Danburn? Wish I could have known him earlier, before all this." Rett said that he did as well. "Kendrick has been helping me find a place to stay. I know you said I could be there with you, and I will for a little while, but after being in prison for so long, I just want to have my own space, a place I can come and go from when I please."

"I understand." He did too, more than his dad would realize. "When I left home and went to college, I was surprised by the freedom I had. I think that's why I messed up so badly that first year. I had no idea how to be my own man."

"You've done well. And now here you are, the mayor of your fine city. I couldn't be prouder of you, Rett. Not one bit." He nodded and hugged his dad to him.

Their hug had been heartbreaking that first time. His dad had cringed away from him then, but he was getting better. He'd explained why he'd done that, been afraid of him.

"Men where I was, they don't touch in a friendly way. No hugging, unless you wanted a shiv in your back. There wasn't any touching at all, not if you didn't want to get it in your backside." His dad's face flamed up bright red. "I'm sorry. That was crude. I'll get used to you again, this being a dad and all."

The courtroom was called to order, and as they were being seated again, Rett looked around the room. It was a typical area, he thought, but with one major change. Like his offices on the second floor, this one was in an old school house, and had at one time been the cafeteria. Old chalkboards still hung on the walls, as well as a primer for the written alphabet that was behind the head of the judge. It was quaintly bizarre, Rett thought. And only something that could happen in a small town.

The judge got everyone settled and his mom was brought in. She had not done any better in jail than his dad had. And for as much as he wanted to say he was glad, she was still his mother and he felt horrible for her. Not enough to get her out, but enough that he felt badly.

It took another twenty minutes to get her calmed down. She was pissed about being in jail. The conditions were not up to par, and was upset that anyone would think she was a terrible enough person to put behind bars. The judge told her three times to hush and listen, but his mother thought, as usual, it was her way or none at all.

"I will not hush. I'm a grown woman and I demand that you take these chains off and allow me to go. There is no reason whatsoever that I should be treated like this." The judge, Malcom Wilson, opened her file that had been handed to him. But before he could speak, Mother started talking again. "If you're not going to do as I say, then I want a lawyer that knows his business. I'm going to own this little town when this is over, just you wait and see."

The gavel came down hard on the desk, making not just Rett jump, but about four of the jurors and the officer that was at the door. Then Malcom, a man that was usually full of humor and good graces, stood up and leaned over the large podium that he was behind.

"You will shut your mouth right now or I will put a gag on you. Not an order for one, but a gag that will give each and every one of us some peace and quiet. Good Christ, woman, no wonder I can't get anyone to keep an eye on you. You're noxious to the ear." His mom opened her mouth to no doubt come back with something caustic when Malcom spoke again. "Mrs. Welsh, I have a big supply of furnace tape right here that I ain't afraid to use. I will—and I swear this to you—cover your mouth up so tight your poor tongue will think you've died it'll have so much rest."

Rett laughed. So did his father, causing his mother to turn and look at them both. Rett knew the exact moment that she realized that her husband was free and enjoying her being reprimanded.

"What is he doing out? I thought I made it perfectly clear to you, Everette, that you were not to have any contact with him. And here you sit, chumming it up as if he was special. Well, he's not. He's a murderer, and I want him gone." She turned to the judge. "You can't let him out of prison. I demand that you put him back. I like being in my house alone. He was nothing more than a pain in my bottom while he was there, and I have things the way that I want them."

"Well, ain't that just too bad? Come to find out, he ain't no more a murderer than I am. You went and set him up, didn't you?" His mother huffed and told him he was wrong. "We found that not only did you lie to the police, but you threatened this poor man, your own husband, into lying for you so that you'd not have to go to jail."

"I have no idea what you're talking about. My husband does not deserve to be out of jail. I told you, I liked him there. He's not in my way for the things I want to do." Malcom looked in Rett's direction. He wasn't sure if he was looking at him or his dad, but he could see pity there. And shock.

Then his dad stood up. Rett stood with him, not sure what

was going to happen or what he would say, but he'd stand with and beside him no matter what it was.

"Your honor, I've been in that prison for a long time. A good while for a crime I didn't commit. I missed my son, him becoming a man of worth, as well as being free. That was something I missed a great deal." Malcom sat down as Dad continued. "I was drunk, yes sir, I'll tell you I was at that. But I wasn't at the wheel when it crashed into those poor people. My wife was. She was hollering at me about how I had shamed her. She'd gone on about how our son was never going to amount to nothing, and that she hated me. And she then put me out on the side of the road. You might say she was more than a little distracted, but that sure isn't any excuse."

"I was nowhere near him when he killed those people." His mom turned to Malcom. "I just don't know where he's coming up with this. You have two witnesses that say they saw me at my home. One that I live in without any people to bother me."

Malcom asked the attorneys if they were ready. Both of them nodded. "Then let's get this here thing going before she goes and does all the work for you. Damn, but I sure wish I could represent the other side in this. Damn it all to hell."

Rett had to hand it to the attorney that was seated next to his mother…she not only kept her in line, but quiet too. Not to say there weren't some outbursts, several of them as a matter of fact, when her charges were brought up. But she sat there with her hands gripping each other while occasionally turning and glaring at them.

Rett watched and waited with his dad. There were times when he was sure that his father was hurt more than he was showing. More than once he'd requested to be excused and made his way out of the courtroom. When he'd asked if he wanted him to go, his dad said that he only needed a few moments. Then he would return, his face a mask of resolve as the proceedings continued.

The day ended with his mom being taken back to jail. His father, exhausted he knew from the ordeal, asked if he might go home now. Rett sat there in the courtroom alone, and thought of his mother and dad.

When he'd been smaller, just about nine or ten, he knew that his mother was controlling. But like his dad, he had also found it easier to just do what she wanted rather than to go against her. She was a force, it seemed, that few people would come out on top after talking to. And if someone did happen to win, it was a small victory, as she'd eventually get back at the person.

Rett thought of the paperboy that used to deliver their newspaper every day. She'd told him to stop putting the paper in the box at the end of their driveway and for him to bring it up to the door. She'd wanted him to hand deliver it, to knock on the door and give it to her. This went on for an entire summer, and no amount of calls made to the newspaper would make the young boy do as she wanted. Even calls to his parents didn't go as she had demanded, until one day the paperboy was nearly killed.

Even as a child no older than the youngster, Rett knew his mother had done it. The boy — and his name would forever be burned into his mind — David Cody, had been beaten close to death, his back broken in two places, as well as his head bashed almost open. And after such a horrific beating, he'd lain where he'd been hurt, a back alley behind the supermarket, all night, with no one to help or get him much needed help.

After that, no one would deliver anything to their door. Not a package came to their house, no flowers were brought had there been anyone to send them. Nor was their mail even left in the box. Everyone in their town, from the chief of police to the next kid who would be on their route, knew that his mom was a horrible person and avoided her and their home.

That was the sort of person his mother was. Mean, manipulative, and abusive to anyone who disagreed with her. Rett wondered what she'd done to his dad to make him say he was the one driving that night.

CHAPTER 11

Cassie was at her desk when someone came into her office. She'd only just gotten it set up. Things were yet to be hung on the walls, pictures and other items, but she loved the way it turned out. And the desk from Danburn and Kendrick was beautiful. The man smiled at her, not hiding this fangs from her at all.

"I wanted to show you that we're not going to keep secrets." She nodded and felt her dragon move along her skin. "Good. You know what I am, I know what you are. My name is Phillip Markum. I'm one of the doctors that Pierce Cunningham asked to come here and help out."

"No one mentioned that you'd be stopping by." She glanced at her computer and saw that there were no new messages since earlier. "I don't know anything about you."

"That's right. And I don't know you either. I told Pierce that I'd not take the job. That it's…. Well, it's been very hard for me the last decade or so, and I told him no. But I got to thinking about it, what it might be like to be a physician again, and I thought I'd come here, just to talk to you." Cassie asked him what had happened. "Right, no secrets. My mate was killed. Murdered really. And as most would, I imagine, I decided that I was finished with the world."

"And now you're not?" He grinned at her. "I still don't know why you're taking this job. Perhaps we should begin there."

"Of course. Why I'm taking this job. As I said, I wasn't going to. But then I came around. Not inside, but from watching the people going in and out of here. They're happier. I mean, some of them seemed like there would be no changing their outlook on life, but they were excited about having this place." She asked him why that was important. "Because I thought that if I was able to help put a few more smiles on some of their faces, that I'd feel better too."

"It's more than that though, isn't it?" He nodded but didn't speak. "I don't know anything about you. And in the event that you missed something lately with your checking us out, we had a bit of trouble with our last in house doctor. He decided to make this place his own little blood machine."

"Yes, I heard. And the way that it was dealt with, the way that you took care of not just what was going on but the vampire involved, showed me that this is a place that I can work in." She told him she wasn't sure how the vampire was dealt with. "His maker killed him. It wasn't really as cut and dried as all that. I made sure that he got to tell his side of things. That he knew what he'd done was wrong. And so you know, his wealth has been put into an account to pay to any families that might still be around. If not, then the money — and there is a great deal of it — can be used here. For whatever you wish."

"You were his maker?" He nodded once, the finality of

it making her think he didn't wish to discuss it any more. "Back to you working here...you know that I have no say whatsoever about that. I'm running the place, but I have no more knowledge about what you might be doing here than I would being a pack leader."

"I'm aware of that. And I thank you." He didn't elaborate, so she assumed he meant for the change of subject. "I'll talk with Pierce today. Also Lord Danburn. I'm to understand that his mate is the one that is funding most of this project."

"You don't approve? Of a woman that is in charge?" He asked her what she meant. "I don't know. Most men, especially ones your age or older, seem to think a woman is only good for one thing."

"Your father." She wasn't sure how he knew about him, but nodded. "He's not a man that I would want to be compared to. I'm to understand that you have...how shall I say this? You have tangled with him recently."

"I retrieved something he had that belonged to me." Phillip laughed and told her that wasn't all she'd done. "I don't know what happened to him when I arrived. It was.... It felt like I was gaining strength as he lost his. I figured it had something to do with the book I had."

"It was. The book and all that surround it belong to you. Your mother was extremely smart in the things she did to keep it safe." Cassie told him that she thought so too. "I would like to tell you my plans, if you have time to listen."

"I'm just getting set up here having only been put in charge recently." He nodded, but there was a look, one that she chose to ignore. "I will say this much; you'll not use this as a feeding ground for you or any of your friends. I'll burn you at the stake or whatever else you happen to be next to should I find out that you are."

"As you should. And I won't. Never. I am at an age where I don't have to feed as often. Not to say that I don't, but I promise you this on my life…no one here will ever have cause to think I will do them harm. Unless it is to save you or any of the rest of the dragons. Mates included."

"Why are you coming back? Is it because you feel that you're somehow responsible for what Walter did? You don't have to. As you said, he's been taken care of." He said that was part of it. "And the rest? If it's all the same to you, I don't want someone working here because they think to be a martyr. These people have enough to deal with without someone bringing them down all the time."

He laughed. It was hearty and full of good humor. She could also tell that it had been a while, a long one, since he'd done that…laughed for a good reason. Whatever his reasoning was.

"You are refreshingly honest and forthcoming. I think, more than anything, I will enjoy coming here to see what you might have to say. I'm sure that it will tickle me in some way. Even if it's to be pissy with me." He stood up and she did as well. "It will be a great pleasure working beside you, Lady Cassie. Very much so."

After he left she decided to see what she could find on the vampire. She knew that she'd not find the entire story. He had been around for centuries and the Internet had not. So as she searched for his name, she found out about his mate. Margo Markum had not met her end well, it looked like.

She knew that things like this, a death of a mate, could

turn any supernatural into something different. Most, as was her experience, went bad, killing anything that crossed their paths. Some, very few that she knew of, turned their life around and tried to move on. She had a feeling that Phillip was one of those uncommon people.

He'd been a very successful surgeon. A great doctor, and had had an office not far from here. Phillip and his wife had donated a lot of money and time to a great many charities as well, most dealing with orphaned children whose parents had died from drugs or sexually transmitted diseases. She was just pulling up an article on his wife when she felt a kind of tightening in the air. She stood up when she saw Phillip in her office again.

"Come with me." She nodded. It was probably foolhardy, but she knew that whatever had brought him here was bad. "Close your eyes."

As soon as he wrapped his arms around her, she felt the whoosh of air envelope her. When they stilled, she opened her eyes again and stood still when he told her to. Her father was in his chair where she'd left him yesterday, and he was talking to a man that she did not know.

"He has your mate. They cannot see or hear us, but please remain still. I cannot hold us both long if you move." Nodding, she asked him what they were doing here and where Rett was. "I do not know. I only know the man across from your father and his deed. Where the young human is, I have yet to figure out."

"Is he all right?" Phillip said that he was, thanks to her. "The dragons, they gave him a lot of power."

"They have saved his life because you are his. Do not be

167

fooled by the way your mate recovered. He was only down for a few hours, but in that time, he changed in more ways than just his strength. Rett is very powerful, but does not know it as yet." She nodded when Phillip told her to listen. "When we are told where young Rett is, I'll go for him. You will deal with these two, yes?"

"I will. But how much trouble will I be in when I do?" He laughed softly by her ear. "I'm pretty sure no one will care about my father, but I don't know the other man."

"He is wanted by all manner of agencies that wish him arrested. But I would imagine dead would suit their purposes much better. He must be found." More laughter again. "Do not burn him too badly, my dragon." She listened to her father and this other man while they spoke.

"You look like shit, Arle. What the fuck have you been doing with yourself?" Her father just waved the man off. "Anyway, I have the little fucker. Damn, but you didn't tell me that he was going to be pissy about being caught. Two of my men were killed in the taking of him. And now that he's under lock and key, so to speak, those men, they want more of a piece of him as retribution."

"They can when I have what I want." She was glad to hear that Rett had given as good as he got. But if her father thought they were going to get a second chance then he was stupider than he looked.

"I have things running in the right direction to get the woman. She's been holed up in that office of hers all day. When she leaves, I'll have her as well. What are you going to do with her?"

"Never you mind. But when you get her, make sure that

you keep her in iron. I don't want her getting away because you were lax in what you were to do." Phillip left her to move around the room. But she was to stay still as she listened to her father. "I'm telling you right now, Burt, I don't know what she did to me, but that bitch is proving harder to kill than her mother was."

Her world simply crashed around her. Her dear mother had been killed by this monster. She'd known it, of course, but to have him admit it was just too much. And now he was going to do the same to her if given half a chance. Before she could move to kill him, the door crashed open, hitting the wall hard enough to shake pictures and knock glasses off the shelf.

~~~

Danburn watched his friend carefully. He knew that he was not only suffering from the aches and pains of his ordeal, but also what he'd done. More importantly, he supposed, was how he'd killed another human being.

"Are you all right?" Rett looked up at him and nodded, then shook his head. "I would imagine that is how I would feel if it happened to me. No one blames you for this, Rett. What you did was justifiable."

"Justifiable or not, I killed a man. Those dragons? They helped me escape. I mean, Christ, Danburn, they just came right out of my body and helped me to get out of there." Danburn sat down and waited. He knew that Rett wasn't used to any of this, and had to work through what he'd done. "I was sitting there, just trying to figure out my fate, which I imagined wasn't all that good, and they were there. No pain this time, just like a gentle breeze over my body. The bigger one, Agnus—I have named them, by the way—Agnus asked me to put out my hands and she flamed the bonds off, not once scorching me or even making me hot. Then when I was free of those, they guided me to this house. I'm guessing they knew where Cassie was because they're a part of her."

"They're a part of you as well, Rett, and knew that you needed to help her. From what I understand, Cassie was pretty much out of it. He admitted it; Cassie's father admitted to killing her mother. That alone would have gotten him brought before me. His sentencing would have been far worse had that happened." Rett said that he wasn't helping. "I'm trying to. I just wanted you to know that what you did, how you ended his life, was a great deal more merciful than I would have been."

"The house was so quiet. I thought for sure that they'd brought me to the wrong one. And I understood them. Just like you and I are talking now, I knew what they said. Go this way. Turn here. Then we were standing right outside the room they were in." Rett looked at the house from where they were sitting. There were people around the house...firemen, police, and a few neighbors. Most, it seemed, felt like he did. Good riddance to the occupant of the house. Danburn shifted on his butt. The ground was dry but a little cold, though he doubted that Rett felt it. "I heard them talking, the man and what I only assumed then was her dad. I heard Arlington say that he was going to kill my Cassie as he had her mother. It's what...I guess you can say that it filled me with such a rage that I think the dragons felt it as well."

Danburn asked him what he'd done. Rett sat there for several moments, gathering his thoughts, Danburn knew. What he'd done, how they both had ended this, was nothing short of magical.

"I saw Burt first. The dragons were with Cassie and I saw him drawing a gun. I have no idea if he was going to shoot her or the dragons, but I had to do something. I just jumped on him. I mean, literally jumped on his back when he stood up, and I grabbed his head. Turning it like I did, it wasn't as hard as I thought it would be. I heard it too, the crack of his neck breaking, then I let him go." He looked at Danburn then. "I felt it, the power of love. I know that sounds so bizarre, but I honestly felt my love for Cassie surround me. I saw her then."

Burt James had been killed instantly, his neck broken by Rett, he knew now. The amount of strength, the control that one had to have to pull off such a feat, had the police shaking their heads. Danburn knew, as he was sure that most others did, it wasn't adrenaline that had made him superhuman to do something like that, but that he was more powerful than most paranormals now.

"I knew that she needed my help. I had no idea how... perhaps it was the dragons. She was screaming at her father. Telling him that he'd killed her mother for no reason other than greed. Then he...I think he was going to shift and kill us both, but suddenly this knife was in my hands. It was hard and long, and I knew just what I had to do with it. I threw it... Danburn, you would have thought I was one of those carnival guys throwing knives at his wife. But it hit him in the face, his eye, and seemed to slow his movements, like he was frozen in pain. It was then that Cassie touched him. When she did that, he fell back and the dragons entered her body, and I knew that she was hot, like dragon's breath. It just seemed the most natural thing in the world for me to wrap her into my arms

171

and lend her my strength too." Danburn looked at Rett when he turned to him. He was haunted…it was the only way he knew to describe what he saw in his face. "The knife that I threw at Arlington when I got in there, do you know where that came from?"

"Yes." Rett didn't seem to require an answer, so he didn't provide him with one. The knife, made of the purest iron that he'd ever seen, had been given to Danburn as a gift more centuries ago than he could even recall. How it had gotten to Rett, just when he needed it, was a mystery. Danburn wondered if it was the dragons, and felt that was the right answer. "The dragons helped you there as well, I believe. He wouldn't have gone down easily, not one of his age. But the blade that you slammed into his face kept him from shifting and harming the two of you. And that was what allowed Cassie to finish him off. It had to be done."

"He spoke to me. With the knife in his face, he talked to me about what he was going to do once he was freed. And the things he was going to do to Cassie. He meant to make her suffer because of what he felt she'd done to him over this book. All this because of some rules in a book that was meant to make their kind safer." Danburn told Rett that people had done far worse for a great deal less. "Yes, I guess. But he was going to hurt what was mine. When he realized what was being done to him, how we were…I guess how we were killing him, he started screaming. I thought at first it was him trying to get away. But it was pain. Blood started pouring from his eyes and nose at first. Then his ears. His face blistered, along with his hands. We were cooking him, I think. His hands melted, just fell from his wrists, his legs bloated until they burst under his clothing, and the putrid smell of rot was around the room. It was his face that will haunt me forever. The way his one good eye burst in the socket, his lips slid from his mouth. I watched as his nose and ears just fell away, joining the rest of his parts on the floor. But we didn't stop. I think we both knew that to do so would have meant our deaths. Then when he was dead.... After we killed him, we—with the help of the dragons—brought his body out. The dragons said it would explain a great deal to the police."

The book was gone. Danburn had a feeling Cassie had it. He wasn't sure, but he thought that she'd hidden it away before today. He looked over at the house as the fire department simply stood back and let it burn. They were keeping the fire under control, but there was little help for trying to save it. Not that he thought anyone cared to.

When Cassie joined Rett on the ground, Danburn got up to leave them to deal with all this. But before he could move much more than a few feet away, Cassie called him back. He stood before her as she stared at the ground. Danburn had a feeling he knew what she was going to say.

"We had to bring out the bodies so that they'd find them. Phillip, your friend, said it would be the only way that anyone would acknowledge their deaths. That it was important that people knew. The house fire was started afterwards. I did it." He nodded. "I know what I did was wrong. And so you know, Rett was only involved because of his association with me. The dragons that.... Mine are the ones that helped him."

"You think you would have done any less for him should the roles have been reversed?" She shook her head. "Then I see no reason for you to entertain any belief for me to hold

173

you responsible for any of this. If that is what you're saying to me now. As far as I'm concerned, you did the world a favor by killing both men. I'm sure there will be a great deal more closure for a lot of people now."

"He killed my mother." Danburn said he knew that now. "Killed her because she was powerful and clever enough to use what she had to keep the world a better place. And he hated us both for that. Because we were smarter and stronger than he was."

"I think your mother would have been very proud of you both today. I know that I am. What you did here today, all of this, it shows me what a wonderfully caring person you are. And strong. I won't piss you off, and I doubt anyone will try again to do what your father did." She looked up at him as Rett took her hand in his. "The deaths will be written down as accidents. Murder suicide that was caused over a gambling debt. Phillip took care of that. The bodies will be taken to the morgue, and then later buried."

"Thank you." Danburn nodded, but before he could turn to leave Cassie spoke again. "I have the book. I would like for you to have it. I know that there is a way for you to keep it hidden away."

"I do. But are you sure?" She said that she was, more than anything else. "Then I shall take it and put it in a safe place for you."

He made his way to the bodies that had been covered by a sheet. The humans here would know nothing of what was laying before them. They saw two men, one with his neck broken, the other burned badly. Danburn wondered at the control that it would have taken to burn a body the way that she had, but said nothing. He looked at Phillip when he stepped beside him.

"When I went there with her, it was only my intention to find the young man and have her speak with her father. I had hoped that she'd kill Burt James, but I believe hearing what she did from her father shocked her." Danburn said that it would have him as well. "When Rett came in and killed James, just leapt upon him and broke his neck...I have to tell you, Danburn, I've never been so terrified and proud at the same time like that. Doubtful that I ever will be again."

"And Arlington? Cassie hasn't said, but I believe it was her that killed him. I would imagine that she was given little to no choice in the matter." He looked at Phillip when he didn't answer right away. "The knife that Rett had, do you know how he got it from my safe? Did you do that?"

"I didn't, as a matter of fact. They did." They looked over at the tree line at the nine dragons there, standing guard, he thought, over their hosts. With Cassie coming to her own magic, her dragons had grown and multiplied as well. "She killed her father, Danburn. The calmness, the way that she simply did it, was controlled and emotionless. The blade that Rett used slowed him, but she did it. The power radiating from her...well, I hate to admit this even to you, but I had to go and feed afterwards. It was like the heat of ten suns on my skin. Danburn, she burned him from the inside out. I would bet that should he be cut open for an autopsy, they'd find nothing but ash."

"Anger. Love. Hurt. I would think those things were what gave her such power, wouldn't you?" Phillip said that he thought so, but also something more. "Her mother."

"Yes. I think in some way she was there too." Phillip shivered. "Cassie didn't shift. I fully expected her to do so, turn into herself and kill him. But she only touched her fingers to his body and...Christ, the screams. I doubt I'll sleep well for a month for fear of hearing him begging for his life as she killed him. And Rett? He held her in his arms, as if feeding her some of what he was so that she could end this."

Danburn was sure that was what had happened. That the two of them, in anger, had not just killed Arlington, but had made him suffer in the most heinous way ever. Danburn was going to have to make sure that the two of them really believed they'd done the right thing. For a great many people. He wondered how long it would be before they saw it that way too.

Phillip asked him about the job at the shelter. He told him what he knew, regarding the pay, benefits, as well as what would be expected of him. Phillip said that he needed neither the benefits nor the pay, but he would take the job.

"You want to work for Cassie?" He said that he wanted to work with her, not for her. "Well, I'm sure that she'll see it as her working for you, but you can try that route."

They both laughed. Danburn wasn't sure, but he thought that those two would make a great team. And that Rett would be the best mayor the town ever had as well.

CHAPTER 12

Elba was going to make them see reason today. She had been shuffled back and forth from the filthy cell to the equally dirty courthouse for days now, and she was frankly getting sick of it. They had to know she'd done nothing wrong, that it had been her husband all along. And the fact that he was sitting there every day, just staring at her as if she had done something bad, was getting on her last nerve. Once she'd convinced him to do as she'd said and take the brunt of this, she'd give him a piece of her mind as well.

"Mrs. Welsh?" Another man in a suit. She was tired of them as well…firing them was annoying. "Mrs. Welsh, my name is Carter Bloom. I've been assigned your case by the county courts. I'd like to go over a few things with you."

"If you want to tell me that I should just plead guilty, then you can take yourself home right now. I didn't do a thing wrong." He said nothing but stared at her. "I want you to go to my husband and tell him that he has to stick to his story. I'm not going to spend time in jail, and he'd better do something about it."

"They have witnesses that state you were not at home

when you said you were. And that your compulsory actions had people lying to the police by blackmail and a hostage situation. There isn't much for me to do other than to try and get you a lower sentence. But I doubt the judge will see it that way, especially in light of how you've conducted yourself in his courtroom." She stood up from her bed and glared at him. "You should know that if you don't take a deal, at least one that will get you a lesser sentence, you're going to lose this case."

"Lose it how? Because you're incompetent? I think that's a given, don't you? But I'm not going to lose because you'll see my husband and tell him that I want him to go back to the way things were before. I don't care for his treatment of me, and I'm finished with him. Also my son. Did you know that he thinks himself a lawyer as well?" He asked her if she meant Rett Welsh, the mayor. "Mayor? You mean that ridiculous story was true? I never told him he could take on a job like that. Is this whole town nuts? He can barely keep me in money; how is he expected to keep this town running? You need to get me out of here. I must get him back to what he was doing before all this as well."

"I'm sorry you feel that way, Mrs. Welsh, but from all accounts, he's done a great job so far." She huffed. "Now. Would you like to talk about a plea bargain for your — ?"

"No, I do not want to talk about a bargain. I'm not on sale, and I don't appreciate you inferring that I'm to be discounted like day old eggs. Your job is to get me out of here, and I expect you to do that today. I have things I need to take care of." He just stared at her, as if she wasn't speaking English. "What is wrong with you?"

"Nothing. But if you think you'll get out of here at all, it's not happening. You're going to prison. And from what I can see here, for a very long time too." Elba asked him what she'd done to deserve that. "Well, for starters, you killed two people. You lied to the court system. Falsely accused someone else of your crimes. Then there is the list of things that you will be tried for in a separate case. Such as your neighbors on either side of you filing a complaint against you that states—"

"I'll take care of my neighbors when you get me out of here. They'll drop their suits quick enough when I have a talk with them." He asked her what she was going to do. "They'll see reason once I see them. And if talking won't work, then I'll have to work on their families. I have my ways. People know better than to make me upset. There are rules, you know. Ways things have to be done, and if they mess with those, then I have to show them the error of their ways. I want you to get me out of here."

"It's not going to happen." Elba asked him what good he was if he wasn't going to do that. "I'm going to try my best to keep you from getting life without parole. You've really done some pretty horrific things to people. That doesn't even count the murder of two innocent people."

"No one is innocent. Everyone has things they've done that they're not proud of. Skeletons in their closets that come back to bite them in the bottom. Perhaps whoever killed these people, they did everyone a favor. Did you ever think of that?" Had she had a camera, she might well have taken his picture. He had the perfect look of shock on his face. "You are surprised I'd think that way? That I know so much about human nature I can hit it so effortlessly like I have?"

179

"No. I'm shocked that you have so little regard for even human decency. When they told me I had to take this case, someone said I'd be better off not being an attorney than to have to deal with you. Christ, I think everyone around you *would* be better off if you were to get life." She told him to watch his language. He laughed. "You want me to watch my language when you murdered two people? I have to tell you, that's probably the stupidest thing I have ever heard."

"I don't want you here any longer." She wanted to get out of there, but she didn't have to put up with people making her upset. The list of things she had to do when someone was smart enough to release her was getting longer and longer. "You're fired."

He just laughed at her. She wanted to tell him that he was on her list, a very long one, but he only saluted her and left. No begging. Nothing said about how he was assigned to her and had to stay. She nearly called him back to ask if he understood that he'd just lost his job when she heard the door open and close at the other end of the hall. Elba sat down and plotted.

She'd always been very good at it. She supposed in a way it was seeking revenge, but she didn't like calling it that. It made her sound as if she wasn't a nice person. She wasn't, but she didn't think she had to announce it to the world. No, she had a certain way that things needed to be done, how others were supposed to act and what consequences were going to be heaped upon them if they detoured from her list. A list she was extremely proud of.

No going against her word on the way things were done. Along with that, there was a sub heading of not disagreeing with anything she wanted. That rule had been the easiest to instill in people. A few well-placed hits with her bat and things went her way.

She didn't want people mentioning her age or appearance, unless it was to tell her how good she looked or on her style. Few people knew how old she was, and she liked it that way. The one time that anyone had dared to comment on her having a senior discount card was no longer able to speak. And she was going to make sure that her son wouldn't be so blunt about it either. The nerve of that boy thinking he could just blurt out her age as if he had a right to.

There were smaller things as well. Ones that her neighbors had tried their very best to get around, but she'd shown them the error of their ways. Her logic on having a well maintained lawn, not too many decorations out when it was some holiday, and most certainly no pagan ones for those that were about death and candy. These rules, all hand written and laminated by herself, were handed out to new people on her street, and also when others somehow forgot them.

"Hello, Elba." She was startled out of her thoughts when she heard her husband speak. He was forever doing that, sneaking up on her when she was doing something important. Not even bothering to stand in his presence, she turned her back to him. "You're mad. I understand that, but you lied to me."

"About what? I don't lie, George, and you know that." He gave her a short burst of laughter that irritated her to no end. "Why are you not in prison? I thought I made it clear that is where you needed to be so that I could go about my business."

"I had business as well. And you told me that you'd make sure that my son would know what you did and why, and that he'd come to visit. He never once came to see me." She didn't bother commenting on such a stupid reason. "He told me the things you said to him. How you told him that you'd tried to make me not drive home. That you thought that I was a drunk and a womanizer as well. None of that is true, Elba, and you know that."

"You never answered me as to why you're out of prison. As I have said, you're supposed to be there for another twenty years." He laughed again. "You won't think this is so funny, George, when I get out of here. I'm going to make sure you understand the meaning of commitment. You were supposed to do as I told you. Committed to it as I wanted. But here you stand on the wrong side of the bars acting like you have all the right in the world to be there. I want you to get me out of here."

"I'm not going to do that, Elba. I won't lie for you again, nor will I do as you tell me. Doing what you wanted has gotten me nothing at all, and I think I like being a free man. Not just from prison, where you put me, but also simply free of you." He laughed again. "Freedom is wonderful. And I've gotten to know my son again and his lovely wife."

"Wife? Well, that's not going to work out for me. How is he supposed to make sure that I have my money each month, as well as him under my thumb, if there is another woman in his life? No, I want you to take care of that right now. Have an affair with her or something so that he can divorce her. I won't have it." George just stood there. "Are you stupid, George? I told you what I wanted and here you just stand. Get to it."

"No. I like her. And I don't think me having an affair with her would even cut it. They're in love. You should be happy for them, not tearing them apart." She started to tell him that it mattered little to her if Rett was happy so long as she was. But George, for the first time in her memory, cut her off. "I'm happy too, in the event you even care. Not that I think you will, but I wanted you to know."

"You're right, I don't care. Nor do I for you thinking you're going to get away with all this. George, I'm very disappointed in you. You've always done what I told you, and now you think just because there is some delay that prevents me from getting out of here that you can be uppity. Well, that's not going to work either. Straighten up or I'll do it for you." George just stood there, acting like she'd not just given him things to do. "I want you to find me a good attorney while you're doing this. One that will do just what I tell him. And you're to make sure that those neighbors know I'm returning as well."

"I'm selling the house. I hated it anyway, and I have no use for it since I'm going to live with Rett and his wife, and then find something of my own that you've not spoiled." She told him he would not. "But I am. Since you're not going to get out anytime soon, I've decided that I want to move on and up with my life. I even have a job. A fun one working in the shelter here in town."

"What is wrong with you? What are you going to do with a job? George, I swear when I'm out, I'm going to have you tested for mental illness. You've lost your ever loving mind if you think I'll allow you to work with those sorts of people." He asked her what sorts she thought they were. "Don't give me that. Lazy people. Uneducated, not to mention unclean. Why, they probably have all kinds of diseases as well. You'll stop this right now. You're only doing it to make me upset. Well, I hope you're happy. You've upset me."

"I don't care." She wanted to smack him. To hurt him as badly as he was her with this talk. "I like it there. And I get to help Cassie, my daughter-in-law. She's someone that I can admire. And Rett loves her very much."

"For now. When I get finished with the two of you, you'll never be able to set foot in any decent place. George, I'm sick of telling you this, but I want you to do as I've said. You need to go back to prison and get me out of here." He said no to her again. "I'm not happy about this. And when I get out, you're going to know it."

"But you're not going to get out. And if I can, I'll help in any way that I can to make sure of that." He smiled at her, one that showed his teeth. "I like you being right where you are, Elba. And I love where I am as well. A happy man. Something that I never was with you."

"Like I care what you feel, George. This is about me, not you. I've had about enough of this feelings thing. You'll do as I tell you, I'm not monkeying around. First and foremost, I want you to go back to prison. I can't do my work if I'm stuck here. I also need for you to…. Where are you going? Get back here right now."

"I'm going home. To one I can be happy in, that you've never tainted with your evilness. And once I have my own place, I'm going to fill it with things that I like and not think of you once while I'm doing it." He paused before leaving the area she'd been confined to. "You should be very happy in prison, Elba. They have all sorts of rules too. None that I'm sure you'll like, but that's not my problem anymore. Also, I wanted to inform you that I've filed for divorce. I think I'll have a nice celebration when it goes through."

"George, get yourself back here right now. You're not going to divorce me unless I say so. George? Get back here now." The door closing behind him made her angry and she shook the bars hard. Of course she wasn't going to allow this. There was no way she was going to be labeled a divorced person. "George."

She had to make a list of things to do, and give one to George. He had to be retrained, she thought, into knowing who was in charge. Taking her seat on the bed again, she wondered what sort of drugs he was on. That had to be it, he was into drugs now. And that woman, Everette's supposed wife, had given them to him. Elba had a lot of work to do when she got out of here.

~~~

George wandered in and out of the shops on the main street as he thought of his wife...soon to be ex-wife. He was thrilled to be able to go where he wanted when he wanted. There was much to see and a great deal more to catch up on. As he entered a small shop that dealt in used items, he saw a chair that he thought would look great in his little office at the shelter.

Cassie had given that to him. Told him that as her assistant he needed his own space. George was going to talk to people who were fresh out of jail, help them adjust to life on the outside. She said that his perspective on being out would be helpful for them. He'd been sure that he'd only make matters worse when he sat down with his first client.

"I don't think I can make it." George told the man he'd

been feeling that lately as well. "It's too much, all this going on. When I went in, there was only one kind of phone and you didn't carry it around with you."

"I had one when I went in. Of course they took it from me, but I did miss it. Mostly for the way I could just call my son when I wanted to talk to him." The man had told him that he missed his daughter's wedding and other things. "That'll happen. I'm not saying it's a good thing, but you mess up, you gotta expect to pay with some pretty hefty fines."

They had talked for over two hours. Nothing really earthshattering, but just things that they might have been able to participate in had they made better choices. When he left his office, George thought perhaps talking to the stranger had made him realize a great many things as well. That he was a worthy human being.

"Everything is marked down." He turned to the woman that he'd seen around town. "I'm closing up shop. So everything must go."

"I'm sorry." She shrugged, but he could see that it hurt her to be doing this. "Did you lose your lease or something?"

"No. I just wasn't able to make it work for me. Happens, I guess. But when you run and own your own shop, it's a bit hard to go out and get things to put in it. I can't be two people." He wanted to hug her for all the pain in her voice. "My kids are forever telling me that they knew I was going to fail at this. I guess they were right."

"No, no they're not. I have some time on my hands. I'd love to help you out." She told him it wasn't necessary. "But it is. Not just for you, but for me as well. My name is George Welsh, by the way. You're Brenda, right?"

"Yes, Brenda Wright. I've seen you around. Your son, he's the new mayor." George felt the pride in his son shine over him. "He's a good man. Did he send you here? I talked to him a few days ago when he was around. I think he was sad that I wasn't going to make it."

"You will. And no, he didn't send me. I was just getting a little bit of air." She showed him around the store, pointing out things that she'd gotten here and there. "I have a house full of things I want to get rid of. You could bring it here. I've decided to start fresh."

"You don't have to do that, George. I'm sure I'm in over my head anyway." He walked around with her some more, his mind buzzing with the idea of selling his crap off here. "My oldest son, he seems to think that I've been a failure all my life. And for every single time I've helped him out of this or that, he points out how many times I didn't. I swear, it's like he has these blinders on about how much I do for him and the others. Just last month I bought him a baby bed, rocker, and car seat for his new daughter. And do you know what he said about that? He told me that wasn't for him. Who the hell did he think it was for if not for him?"

"I only have the one boy, but I've not had any troubles with him. I have more with my soon to be ex-wife. She's going to prison soon, I hope." He was shocked by what had spilled from his mouth. "I'm sorry. That sounded so horrible."

"No, it's the truth and I'm glad to hear it. It's refreshing and nice of you." He sat in her office and shared a cup of tea with her. "I collect those. Tea cups. I have no idea why, but I love them."

"They're very beautiful." He looked around the office at

the shelf that was filled to nearly overflowing with the delicate little things. "My mother collected tea pots. I have a storage unit filled with them. I'd forgotten about that until just now. I wonder if Cassie would want them. If not, you could sell them for me."

"Really George, it's all right." He said that it wasn't, and she'd be doing him a favor. "I can see what you have. Perhaps it would be better for you to have an auction or something. More of a crowd in that kind of thing."

"I'm in no hurry to make a great deal of money. I have some now." He did too. Danburn had told him that all the money that had been in the joint account Elba had was now his. As well as anything they found in the home. "It's a house full of things. Three bedrooms of it. Dining room table and the works. I asked Rett if he wanted anything, and we're both glad to be rid of it. No good memories associated with it, I guess."

It was an enjoyable way to spend an afternoon, he realized. Sipping tea with a lovely woman. Talking about their problems and things they wanted to do before they pushed up some daisies. He thought to himself, this was the way things should be between two adults.

"Would you have dinner with me?" He was feeling as shocked as she looked. "I'm sorry. I'm not a man that does that sort of thing. But I would enjoy having a meal with you to continue with what we've been talking about today. I could use a nice lovely evening with good company. And I think you could as well."

He was ready for her to tell him no. That he was rude for asking and for her to point out that he was still a married man.

George was ready to get up and leave, tell her how sorry he was for what he'd ruined, when she laughed. He wasn't sure, but he thought that stung a little more than it should have.

"I'd love it." He asked her what she meant. "To go out to dinner with you. I think I would enjoy that very much. And like you said, it's been so nice just talking about nothing at all and not worrying about.... Well, just worrying. I'd love to go to dinner with you. But not as a date. I pay my way and you yours."

"All right. I'm not sure how I feel about letting you pay since I asked you out, however." He watched her face and decided that it was lovely as well. Just too pretty to make sad. "I tell you what, you cover the next time. If you want to see me after tonight. I asked, it's only right that I pay this time."

After they made arrangements — where to go, who was picking up who — he made his way home. He had no car nor a driver's license, so he agreed for her to be their driver. George pulled out his brand new cell phone to tell his son what he'd done. He was almost afraid that he'd tell him he was a fool. George should have known better.

"That's wonderful, Dad. I know you'll have the best time." He was both pleased and touched that Rett seemed to only want the best for him. "Cassie and I are going to clean out the warehouse on Tenth tomorrow. We don't have any idea what her dad might have left her. We already decided to see if Brenda would take it on. You have a good time and I'll see you soon."

George's steps felt lighter, his mood the best, and he was happy, really happy, for the first time in nearly forty years. He figured he was due for a little of his own kind of goodness.

189

He'd given a great deal of it, almost the same forty years, to a lying conniving bit of a woman that he just then decided that he hadn't loved for a very long time. If ever.

CHAPTER 13

Danburn picked up his office phone just as it rang for the third time. He was in a hurry tonight. His wife was going to meet him in town for dinner, then they were going to come back here and take to the skies. Well, he was, with her in his arms, but to him it was as if they were flying together. He heard the laughter at the other end of the call when he barked his name into the thing.

"You always did have a lousy disposition. I guess you've not improved much over the decades, have you, Danburn?" He sat down, the smile at hearing from this particular man making him feel pretty good. "How the hell are you, Dragon King?"

"King, huh? Last time I talked to you, you called me a sub pervert, I believe. Whatever the hell that means." Hanson laughed. "You still trying to become the only dragon on this earth to have sired more children than anyone? I guess you figured out that it's not going to happen for you. Children of our kind can only be birthed by one female."

"Yeah, sucks that. But I'm sort of glad for it. Can you imagine how much I'd be paying in child support right now?

Boggles the mind." They both laughed. "Really, how are you, Danburn? I heard about your dad. I'm so sorry about that. He was a great man, and couldn't have been a better father to me either."

"He loved you like a son, Hanson, you know that. Mom loves you as well. We miss you. Tell me you're coming for a visit." He said that was the plan. "Good, when can I expect you? I'll have your old rooms aired out and ready for you."

"I'm a few days out from there. I've had to go to my own home and clean up a mess. My parents are gone. Not dead, more's the pity, but they left here. The house and surrounding acres were about to be sold off but for the call I got from the bank." Danburn told him he was sorry. "Me too. But it's all going better now. I paid the taxes, and because of that, it's all in my name now. I'm betting that they'll be back since there isn't anybody coming after them for back taxes and shit, but I've got that covered as well."

Danburn had spoken to the McClains a few times over the years. He'd never cared for them. They were the kind of people that thought the world owed them, much like Rett's mother did. But in their case, when they didn't get what they wanted, they would simply burn down the houses and barns of those that had slighted them in some way. And Danburn's mother had absolutely loathed the couple because of their disregard for their son.

"How long can you stay this time? I have a wife now. And Rett is here too." He laughed and so did Danburn. The trouble that the six of them, other men he'd met in college, had gotten into was legendary. "And Mom will be back in a week. She finally went on that cruise I got her for her birthday."

"I'll be there for a little while." Danburn heard it then, something off in his friend's voice. "Don't ask. Not now, if you don't mind. I have a lot of shit going on here, and I can't.... There isn't any way to talk about it over the phone. It's just…I can't, okay?"

"Yes. I'm sorry. I don't know what it is, but I'm sorry." He thanked him and Danburn felt his dragon stir, as if wanting to protect the other man. "You come here, we'll hit the skies and have some fun. Oh, Rett's mate is a dragon too. She's sweet, you'll like her as well."

"I'm sure I will. I want to meet them all, but I really just want to talk to you. Nothing important, just chatting." Danburn said he was there for him. "I know you are. You' always have been. I'll be there in a couple of weeks. Then we'll get into some trouble like old times."

After he hung up, Danburn called in a couple more of his friends, dragons he had known nearly all his life, and asked them to come home as well. Dana and Griffith said they'd be there in a few days, but Kip was a little harder to get in touch with.

After leaving messages in several places for Kip to call him back, Danburn headed out the door again. He was nearly to his car when his cell rang. Kip Newton was never one to be quiet when talking at the top of his lungs got him more attention. Danburn pulled the phone from his ear when he started talking.

"How the fuck are you, buddy?" Laughing, Danburn told him the same thing he'd told Hanson. "Come there? To hang out with the best man I know? Hell yeah, I'll be there. But it will take me a few weeks. I got me a handle on some things here that will make your dick hard."

"My dick is just fine the way it is, thank you." He told him what he thought about Hanson and wanting to cheer him up a little. "I invited Dana Blankenship and Griffith Farley too. You remember them, don't you?"

"Of course I do. I saw Dana a few years back. I've not seen Griffith in a long time. You think Hanson is having trouble with his family again? I heard that they had been brought before the Dragon Tribunal a few years ago. Something about their staff or the like. I never cared for them."

"Me either. And Mom will shit when she finds out they're giving him a hard time, if that's what it is." Kip said he'd bet anything that it was. "I think so as well. It's a shame, really. Hanson is such a great guy."

"He's never been happy since his sister died. I think that changed him more than anyone thought it would. I know that she was sickly and all, but that had to be hard on him to lose a twin like that." Danburn had never met the sister, but he'd heard a great deal about her. "We'll get him fixed up. And then we'll have to see what kind of trouble we can get into."

"Yeah, we'll do that. I'm going to have the house opened up completely, and if I can manage it, I'll to make sure you all stay here for the holidays. Both Thanksgiving and Christmas." Kip said it was a date. "Good. I'll see you soon."

Kissing Kendrick when he finally got to her, he held her tightly in his arms. He loved this woman. With all that he was. He lifted her chin up to look at her when she sighed heavily. Asking her what was wrong, she pulled away and he let her.

"I don't know how to start." He said the beginning would be nice. "Okay, but I think you should sit down. I'm not sure

I want you up and about when I tell you."

"Now I'm afraid." She nodded to the chair. "Just tell me, Kendrick. Whatever it is, we can work it out. And if we can't, I'll fix it."

"You can't fix this. It's set already." He nodded and took the chair. "I told you the other day that I'd read up on dragons and other faerie stories, right?"

"Yes. Mom said she gave you several books. I think there are more if you want. I'd have to find them in the library, but there are a few." She told him she'd already found them. "What is it, love? You're making me nervous."

"I'm going to have a baby. I wasn't sure at first if that was what I'd have, but apparently it is. I went to see a doctor... Danburn, are you all right?"

He looked at her...he could hear her, but not really what she was saying for the buzzing in his ears. Baby? His mind was centered on that single word. A baby? He was going to be a dad? He stood up when she moved to the other side of the room. It was then that he realized she was crying, sobbing really.

"Honey?" She turned on him in an instant. Danburn took a step back, her fury at something almost palpable. "What is it?"

"You aren't happy." He started to tell her that he was when she launched at him again. "What did you expect to happen, huh? That we could go on having sex all the time and no baby would come of it? You told me that you wanted children and now you're backing out. Well, I have news for you, buster... I'm having this baby, and you can go fuck yourself."

"I love you." She stopped with her open mouth to continue

blasting him. "With all that I am, I love you. And I'm so happy about the baby that I could.... Hell, Kendrick, I have no idea what do to, I'm so excited. A baby? You have no idea how.... Christ, I love you."

"I love you too. Are you really happy?" He kissed her. He figured that was the best way of confirming that he did indeed love her. Not to mention, it kept him from breaking down in sobs of joy. "Danburn, we're going to have a baby. And it'll be a dragon like you."

"Yes. Oh honey, I love you so very much. More than I can say with words." Danburn held her while he felt the joy of becoming a dad wash over him. A dad. He was going to be the best he could be. "My dad would be so happy. Mom is going to be over the moon with joy too. I'm betting she rushes home from her vacation as soon as we tell her."

"We'll wait then. I was thinking...can she tell?" He said that he hadn't been able to. "Good. Then I think Thanksgiving. It's only a few weeks away, and she'll be home by then. Okay?"

"Yes. I agree. It'll give us a little more time to keep this to ourselves. Is there anything I need to know? I mean, you're all right, aren't you?" She smiled at him. "I love you, Kendrick. I'm so happy for us both."

Danburn thought of all the things he'd have to do now, just to make the house more secure, warmer at nights, and smiled. He was sure that as soon as the earth found out about the babe, if it didn't know already, all the things he'd thought of and more would be taken care of. A new baby, a dragon lord, would be here soon, and he could not be happier.

~~~

Quinn moved up in the line. She felt as if she'd been here

for days instead of the few hours that she knew. Three hours of time seemed small when it might mean she had heat in her house and perhaps a little bit of food on her table over the next few weeks. It had been a rough time lately.

The lady behind the desk yelled "Next" and a woman with her four children made their way to her. After they were seen by this person they'd still have to go through the process of seeing two more, and then have yet another person verify everything that they'd just told the other three. The checking system was overwhelming.

There were nine people in front of her, and a dozen or more behind. Quinn just wanted to have a seat. To put her feet up and maybe even close her eyes for a moment or two. But she had to get this help, if for no other reason than her mom and little sister would have something to eat.

Quinn worked three jobs, two as a waitress and one as a doctor's assistant. They paid well, for the most part anyway, but there were medical bills for her sister and mom's health was poor too. Medications alone nearly ate up all her money, and then there was food and housing. Everything was so expensive lately.

Her turn came finally and she sat down, handing over all the paperwork she was told to bring.

"You're Magdalena Langley?" She told her that was her mother, but she was too ill to come. "And this other person? Carmine? Who is that? Your kid?"

"My sister. When I was in here before, they told me so long as I had a letter from the doctor stating that my mom was too ill to travel, that I could file a claim for her." The woman stared at her as if she was speaking a different language. "She needs medical assistance, as well as some food. They're not making it."

"And you're just expecting the government to pick up the tab on this? Just because you said so?" The hostility in her voice startled Quinn. "There are hundreds of people in here every day, and you just expect me to give you help because you think you deserve it?"

"No. I never said that. I was told that there might be something here for them, and that I could help my mom out by bringing in what was needed. What is your problem?" The woman stood up, so Quinn did as well. "I don't want any trouble. I just wanted to find out if I could get some help for my mom."

A man came to stand by the woman. Quinn didn't move, but she also didn't take her eyes off the counselor. There was something about her, something that made her lash out that Quinn didn't understand. The man seemed nervous, and that didn't make Quinn feel any better about this.

"Is there a problem here?" The counselor told him that she'd been making demands. "Well, that won't do at all."

"No, she wasn't." The lady that had been in front of her with the children stood up...a formidable woman, who looked like she could lift cars for fun. "She just handed in her paperwork and said that her momma was too sick to come in. That one there, she was all over her like it was her business to make her feel bad. There wasn't any cause for it."

"You just shut your mouth before I take your assistance from you too. I don't have time for this shit. These people are sucking us dry." The counselor turned to her as she continued. "You're not to ever come back. You aren't getting shit from me."

The man tried to get her to calm down, at the very least to hush. But she was on a roll it seemed, and started hurling accusations at Quinn like she was milking the system, also saying that Quinn had called her names, made racial slurs. Then she pulled out a gun.

It was over in a matter of seconds. Quinn felt the first bullet enter her arm, the second her leg as the man tried to wrestle the counselor down to the floor. The woman with the children was shot, and Quinn leaped toward the children to protect them. The third bullet ripped through her belly, and that took her under.

Waking in the hospital, Quinn looked around. Her body hurt, her head was spinning. She had no idea how she'd gotten there, nor when. As she tried to sit up, a hand touched her arm and she looked over. The officer there, a woman who looked old enough to be her mom, told her to be still for a bit longer.

"I.... My mom. She's at home alone with my sister." Milly, she told Quinn her name was, said that someone had gone to get her. She was being treated in the next room. "My sister? Where is she?"

"With her. They're both getting the best of care now." Quinn closed her eyes, the pain making itself known. "You go on and rest now. They're in good hands."

Quinn felt her body drifting. The pain was fading away, but a thought kept pushing its way to the front. The other woman, the one with the children. But making her mouth work around the words to form the questions was hard. Milly seemed to understand.

"She took one in the chest. They did all they could for her, but I'm afraid that she didn't make it. Neither did CarolAnn Bishop." She asked who that was. "The woman that shot you all. Self-inflicted. She might have had some issues at home or work, but she took her own life right after she hurt you and killed Mrs. Smith."

Quinn cried. The woman had stood up for her. Made sure that someone knew that she wasn't at fault. And now she was dead. Her children were orphans. All because someone had a bad attitude.

She let the medications — she was sure that was what made her feel this way — take her under. Quinn felt the softening as some of the pain in her body went away. But the pain in her heart was there still, and she thought it might be for some time.

The next time she woke she was in a different place. The room was softer; the curtains were not sheer as they'd been before. Quinn thought she was in an actual room now, and not the emergency room. As she lay there, her body aching but no longer as painfully as before, she realized that her mom was sitting next to the bed and her sister was asleep in her lap.

Quinn watched them rest. Her mom did look better, but it was hard to make out if that was her drugs or her mom right then. When Mom opened her eyes and looked at her, Quinn smiled and her mother nodded.

"I thought when those police came that you'd been killed or something." Quinn told her mom she was all right. "That woman, she killed herself right after. Another one too, but I don't rightly know what went on there. I'm just so happy that you're all right now."

"I am."

Quinn drifted in and out. Her mom was always there, and her sister would be resting, playing on someone's small computer at times. Quinn wondered what they'd do now. How they'd pay this bill along with everything else. Then there was her missed work.

Things were crumbling around them, bills overdue. Rent as well. There was barely enough for her to support all three of them on what she made, and now she had to add an extensive hospital stay, medications to take at home if they gave her any. As the tears began to flow, she thought of her life and how fucked up it was, and wished, not just for her but for her little family, that things would get better soon.

"Miss Langley?" Quinn opened her eyes again, trying to focus on the face of the man standing in front of her. "Miss Langley, my name is Cooper Frank. I'm with the State Department. I'd like to talk to you about what happened."

He showed her some identification and a badge. It looked official, but she had no way of knowing if it was real or not. Straightening up in the bed, she felt her head swim a little and the pain come back, but he didn't rush her. Instead, he offered to help her should she need it.

"I didn't do anything wrong." He said that he knew that, and asked if he could have a seat. "My mom and sister, they needed some help. I was told by one of the other people at the desk if I had something from the doctor stating that my mom was unable to come there, I could file for her."

"That's right. The agency that you talked with, whoever you worked with, had marked it on her file. There was no reason for things to go the way that they did." Quinn nodded

201

and asked him about Mrs. Smith's family. "Someone is talking to her family now. The children are being cared for by an aunt until we can get them to their father."

"She was so rude...Mrs. Bishop was so angry and rude to me." He nodded again, sadness written all over his face. "I didn't mean to upset her, but I think she was already that when I sat down. I just wanted to get help for my mom."

"That's what I'm here for. We've brought her and your sister to the hospital here, and had them looked over. Your sister is doing well. The medications that she needed are making a great improvement on her pneumonia. But as you know, your mom isn't as easily cared for. Her cancer is really taking its toll." Quinn said she'd been sick for a while now. "Yes. We have the best looking at her, but I'm afraid that there isn't much we can do other than to make her comfortable."

Quinn nodded. The doctors had given her mom six months. It had only been about two, but she could see that she wasn't going to make it as long as they'd given her. Her sister, a small little thing, had gotten sick too, but hers was treatable, with medications that neither of them could afford.

"Thank you for taking care of them. I don't know what I'm going to do about this bill and their getting help, but I'll pay it." He shook his head. "I had insurance, Mr. Frank, but since I've been in here, I'm sure that I've lost my jobs."

"The state is taking care of all your bills, as well as the care for your family. It's the least we can do. Also, a food and medical card has been set up for your mom and sister, as well as you. You've likewise been on the news, and people from all over the world are coming to your aid, and to the family of Mrs. Smith." Quinn told him that wasn't necessary. "Be that as it may, it's done. Your mom is taking care that everyone is thanked. You have a wonderful family, Miss Langley."

"I do. I really do. And I thank you for helping us." He nodded, but didn't speak again. "What about the woman's family, Mrs. Bishop? Are they getting help too?"

He laughed a little, but he seemed surprised by it and smiled as his face turned a slight pinkish color. Mr. Frank thanked her and she asked him for what.

"Mrs. Bishop's family has been in a bit of trouble for a while now. We think, and we're still looking, that was the turning point for her that day. Her oldest son is having some troubles, and we think that might be what triggered her reaction." Quinn said nothing. "I'm sorry about all of this. From the bottom of my heart, I'm so sorry that you were hurt."

"Thank you so much." He nodded. Then the phone near her bed rang. She had no idea who it could be, but assumed it was for Mr. Franks. But when he answered it for her, he handed it to her.

"Quinn? Oh my God, Quinn, I just heard. I'm so sorry love. I'm coming to get you all." Quinn started crying at the sound of her cousin's voice. "We're leaving now. You're going to be staying with us, so I don't want to hear a thing about it."

"I won't. I don't know what we're going to do." She told her they had her now. Between sobs she told her where her mom and sister were. Then when she hung up, Quinn felt like a weight the size of a truck was taken off her shoulders. Mr. Franks asked her if everything was all right. "My cousin, Kendrick, is coming. She just got married to a nice man. They're coming to get us."

"Good for you. That's wonderful news."

After he left, her mom came in with Carmine and she told them what was going on. They were going to have a place to heal. It was all she could think about, how safe they would be with Kendrick. Quinn cried herself to sleep that night, thankful for family. They were all she had—her mom, sister, and now Kendrick—and Quinn was going to be all right for a little while.

Or at least she hoped so.

Before You Go...

HELP AN AUTHOR

write a review

THANK YOU!

Share your voice and help guide other readers to these wonderful books. Even if it's only a line or two your reviews help readers discover the author's books so they can continue creating stories that you'll love. Login to your favorite retailer and leave a review. Thank you.

AWARD WINNING, BESTSELLING AUTHOR

Kathi Barton, winner of the Pinnacle Book Achievement award as well as a best-selling author on Amazon and All Romance books, lives in Nashport, Ohio with her husband Paul. When not creating new worlds and romance, Kathi and her husband enjoy camping and going to auctions. She can also be seen at county fairs with her husband who is an artist and potter.

Her muse, a cross between Jimmy Stewart and Hugh Jackman, brings her stories to life for her readers in a way that has them coming back time and again for more. Her favorite genre is paranormal romance with a great deal of spice. You can visit Kathi online and drop her an email if you'd like. She loves hearing from her fans. aaronskiss@gmail.com.

Follow Kathi on her blog: http://kathisbartonauthor.blogspot.com/

www.ingramcontent.com/pod-product-compliance
Lightning Source LLC
Chambersburg PA
CBHW032127170626
46808CB00006B/2133